CURSE
OF THE
CHOSEN

CURSE
OF THE
CHOSEN

THE ENDARIAN PROPHECY
RICHARD PHILLIPS

47N⬥RTH

Text copyright © 2018 by Richard Phillips
All rights reserved.

Published by 47North, Seattle

www.apub.com

Amazon, the Amazon logo, and 47North are trademarks of Amazon.com, Inc., or its affiliates.

ISBN-13: 9781503949744
ISBN-10: 1503949745

Cover design by Shasti O'Leary Soudant

Printed in the United States of America

I dedicate this novel to my wife and lifelong best friend, Carol.

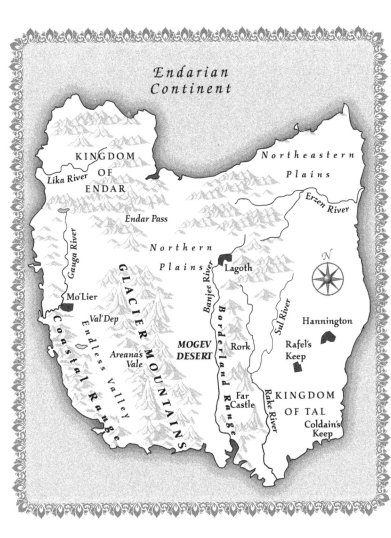

Endarian
Continent

PART I

In the time of supreme danger, when the evil from across the seas draws near, the Chosen shall arise.

—From the *Scroll of Landrel*

1

Kragan stood in the formfitting leather armor that he had come to favor over the black robe worn when his body was human. He towered over Charna. During the months that Kragan's army had been on the march from southeastern Tal toward Endar, the she-vorg had adjusted to his transformation from the horribly scarred Blalock into the seven-foot-tall body with the bronze skin, golden eyes, and fanged mouth. He now shared the body of the strangely seductive primordial Kaleal.

Now Charna, whom Kragan had placed in command of his army, stood by his side, looking through a far-glass at the distant foothills.

"I expect Queen Elan's army to come out of their mountain home to harass us well before we reach Endar," said Charna.

Kragan studied her through his golden eyes, his gaze an ever-present symbol of Kaleal's presence. The stiff breeze from the north whipped Charna's long black hair across her thick shoulders. Her bronze chain mail hung to her thighs, covering the padded leather armor beneath, as her left hand rested on the hilt of the war hammer strapped to her side. Lupine jaws jutted from an otherwise human-looking face, long canines dripping in anticipation of the hunt. Kragan understood just how impatient the commander was to engage the enemy they had marched so far to reach. It was a feeling he shared.

He had waited four centuries to repay these people for isolating him from his homeland that lay beyond the Brinje Ocean. The time-mist they had created a dozen leagues offshore surrounded the Endarian continent. Although ships could sail into and through the mist, centuries passed in the world outside during a single day for those within that fog. More importantly, the mist had disconnected Kragan from his primary source of magic. The Endarian time-shapers had left him a mere shadow of his former self. The memory of what they had done to him stoked a flame in Kragan's chest that would soon burn Endar to dust.

There was a way to disperse this barrier, but that could only be done from within Endar Pass.

Long ago, Landrel, an Endarian wielder of time-shaping and life-shifting magics, had penned a prophecy about Kragan, and Kragan had taken that scroll from the seer's dying hand. After he had examined its contents, the sorcerer wished he had killed the Endarian more slowly. The *Scroll of Landrel* foretold many things that had now come to pass, including the destruction of the kingdom of Tal and the gathering of the army that now spread out below him. But what had vexed Kragan through all the centuries that he possessed the parchment was the description of a young woman prophesied to put an end to his quest for world domination. The scroll had even contained a detailed drawing of the witch.

Though Kragan had known her face, he had not known her identity. That had changed months ago. Her name was Carol, and she was the daughter of High Lord Rafel, the warlord who had fled the kingdom of Tal at the head of his legion, taking more than four thousand of his people across the Mogev Desert and into the lands beyond the Glacier Mountains. The knowledge that Carol had escaped before Kragan had conquered the kingdom in which she had resided infuriated him, but he would deal with the witch in due time.

His thoughts returned to Charna's statement.

"The Endarians will wait for the mountains to channel my army so that they do not have to fight all of the horde at once," he said finally.

"They will keep the bulk of their army back to defend the entrance to Endar Pass," said Charna.

"Yes. But they will send their elite time-mist warriors against us first. Do not take them lightly. We will be fighting in mountains they know thoroughly, and they will have a master time-shaper in support of their defense."

Charna lowered the far-glass, handing it to her aide, who maintained a ready bag of her weapons, helmet, and other tactical gear tied to his horse's saddle. She turned to the west, where the leagues-long lines of her troops marched, the twenty thousand conscripts from Tal at the very front.

Turning to her signal-flag–bearer, she gave the very command that Kragan had been about to utter.

"Signal the double-quick march. I want to be in those foothills before dark."

The vorg raised the flag high, then slapped it down and to the northwest twice in rapid succession. Kragan saw other flag-bearers echo the signal throughout the army. As the lead elements broke into a military jog, the lines of troops stretched out behind them. That was exactly what Kragan wanted. If the Endarian time-mist warriors did make an appearance, the inexperienced Tal conscripts were the ones who would take the brunt of the attack, saving Kragan's vorgish soldiers for the larger battles to come.

Charna swung up onto her black warhorse and thundered down the hill toward the front of Kragan's army, accompanied by her aide and guards.

Before Kragan allowed himself to focus solely on the coming battles, he had one more important task to take care of. Seating himself cross-legged on the ground, he set the fist-size crystal orb half-filled with water on the ground before him. He had long ago distributed duplicates to the most important of his followers who were spread across the continent. Each of the scrying vases contained water drawn from the same pool beneath Lagoth, water extracted by the elemental Boaa.

Stilling his mind, Kragan grabbed control of the water elemental. The fluid inside the clear vase crawled up the sides of the crystalline globe, forming a lens simultaneously mirrored within its twin in the possession of Jorthain, high priest of the protectors. At first Kragan could see nothing, an unusual occurrence that indicated Jorthain must be carrying the orb within his robe's pocket.

"Jorthain!"

The globe transmitted the rumble of Kragan's voice to the water within the vase, and Boaa duplicated the vibration in Jorthain's orb. Kragan saw a sudden light blossom within the globe, along with the image of a hand. Jorthain's skeletal face swam into view.

"What do you desire of me, Lord Kragan?"

The thoughts of Kaleal, the primordial Lord of the Third Deep whose body Kragan shared, rumbled in his mind.

Kragan, you place too much faith in this demigod-worshipping crone. I have little confidence in that fool or his followers.

Kragan's anger crept into his mental response. Since that day when he had made the deal with Kaleal, after having been horribly disfigured by Carol Rafel's magic, Kragan had been subject to the primordial's constraints. Chief among these was the knowledge that Kaleal could undo their partnership should Kragan anger him. The wielder could not allow that until he had killed the prophecy's witch and opened a passage back to his homeland.

Jorthain will accomplish what I need from him, Kragan's thoughts answered.

4

Turning his attention back to the priest, Kragan kept his voice calm. "Tell me that your army is finally on the move."

"We march with the arrival of the equinox," said Jorthain. "And as you directed, I and all of my protectors will travel with our troops. Spring will clear our path toward Rafel's stronghold."

"What is your final troop strength?"

"Just over thirty thousand."

"Make haste. High Lord Rafel has managed to escape from another such army. If he learns the true size of your force, he will abandon his stronghold and flee north to Endar Pass. You will not allow that to happen."

The scowl on the high priest's face told Kragan that he did not like the implied threat. At least Jorthain was not so unwise as to mention his displeasure.

Kragan released Boaa, and the water lens flowed back into the bottom of the scrying vase. Once the army of the protectors had Rafel safely bottled in his canyon stronghold, the hundreds of priests and their forces could throw themselves at Carol Rafel and the rest of the high lord's people at their leisure. And then Kragan and Kaleal could devote their full attention to Endar's destruction.

2

Carol, her brown hair falling over the shirt that hung loosely over her leather riding pants, extended her right hand as a globe of plasma encased it. The ball hissed and crackled, but with her control over the air elemental Putimas, its energy did not harm her. She did not hurl the globe at a distant target. Instead, she spread the plasma so that it crawled up her arm to wrap itself around her body until her torso and legs glowed with a shimmering blue light.

She noticed the tension evident in Arn's stance, smiled at him, and dispelled Putimas, sending the elemental and the effect she had created with it back to its plane of existence.

"You had me worried for a minute," Arn said, releasing a breath.

Carol studied her lover. Two paces tall, he had a rangy build that always seemed coiled to strike. Like hers, his eyes were brown, and his curly hair framed an angular face. Dressed in buckskin, his hand rested on the hilt of the black knife that he had named Slaken. The runes that covered the haft bound powerful elementals within it: Vatra from the plane of fire, Voda from water, Zemlja from earth, and Zrak from the plane of air. Together, they protected the one with whom the blade had made its blood-bond from all elemental magic and its related psychic magic. Only Arn could wield the weapon.

With winter drawing to a close within the sunken valley that the couple had named Misty Hollow, Carol had worked tirelessly to increase the skills with which she wielded her magics. Now, with the approach of the spring equinox and the start of a new year, the thaw would open the paths that led back to their home within Areana's Vale.

She sat down upon a fallen log beside one of the babbling brooks that wound their way through the hollow, and Arn seated himself at her side. The thought of their return to the fortified valley where her father ruled brought forth a flood of memories. The man who sat beside her was the feared assassin known as Blade. Long before he had acquired that reputation, he had been her adopted brother, a troubled teen whom her sire, Rafel, had saved from the gallows and brought into their keep when Arn was twelve. Carol had been only seven.

She had worshipped the young Arn, and that feeling had grown into something far greater. But when she had confessed her love at the age of seventeen, he had gently rejected her advances, leading to an awkwardness that had caused him to leave Rafel's Keep and enter the service of Tal's king, Rodan. After Rodan's death, his petulant son, Gilbert, became king and elevated his favored magic wielder, Blalock, to the role of primary advisor. Together they set out to purge Tal of any lords they deemed a threat to Gilbert's rule. As a test of the loyalty of the king's top assassin, Gilbert sent Blade to kill the family that had taken him in as a boy.

Arn killed the second assassin the king had sent to monitor him and then warned High Lord Rafel of the monarch's order. So Rafel had taken his legion and those who wanted to accompany them and fled into the west, while Arn took a different path. The journey through the borderlands, across the Mogev Desert, and over the Glacier Mountains had taken many months. Along the way, Carol had devoted herself to the study of magic under the tutelage of her mentor and friend, Hawthorne. Blalock attempted to kill her using the fire elemental Jaa'dra. Although she had managed to turn the elemental on Blalock, the experience had left her fire branded, with the image of Jaa'dra intricately etched onto her left shoulder.

Traumatized, she had been unable to cast even the simplest of spells and thus could not assist Hawthorne, who perished combating an unnatural winter storm called forth by Blalock that killed more than two hundred of her people. Soldiering on, Rafel's procession wintered in the Glacier Mountains. But last spring, the high lord's rangers had discovered Areana's Vale, the beautiful, cliff-lined valley where the league of travelers made their home. Unfortunately, the peace her people came to enjoy there would soon be no more, after Carol had regained her magic and killed several of the foul priests who called themselves protectors.

The spell book that Arn had given her—a tome loaded with a trap— had almost robbed her of her sanity as she struggled to understand the mental exercises it called katas. In the depths of her mental illness, her father had turned her over to his high priest, Jason, for treatment. Arn had taken her away from the priests and brought her to Misty Hollow. Here, with Arn's encouragement, she had finally mastered the katas and, in doing so, had unleashed her soul's ability to link with animal minds. She could experience the world through their senses, feel their emotions, and bend their actions to her will.

The addition of these new abilities to her elemental magic skill set gave her hope that she would be able to return to her rightful place among her people and protect them from the storm that was coming.

She felt Arn take her hand and turned to meet his gaze.

"Lost in thought?" he asked.

"Memories of how we came to Areana's Vale. Of the people we brought with us. What naive dreams I had."

"You speak of the philosophy of the outlawed scribe Thorean?"

She sighed. "I hoped that in this new land, I could bring his vision to reality. That I would, in time, help build a new society, where the rights of women and men are equally valued, as they are in Endar. My people once respected me and accepted my guidance."

She blinked away the tears that tried to crawl from her eyes.

"Your loss is my fault," said Arn. "The spell book I gave you almost destroyed your mind."

She leaned over and gently kissed him. "It's okay, my love. Everything valuable comes with a price. If you hadn't brought me here, I never would have had the chance to master the psychic magic the book contained. We'll be needing that knowledge once we return to Areana's Vale."

Arn nodded.

She saw Arn's eyes drift off to the northwest, his lips tightening into a line. She understood the feelings she saw in his face. Spring's arrival would clear the way for the protectors to launch their foul horde at her mountain home. She and Arn needed to get there before their army arrived.

3

Kim's tossing and turning awakened John. He placed a calming hand on her shoulder, and her restlessness subsided.

Outside the window of their cabin, the coming dawn painted the eastern sky above the high cliffs that guarded the valley. By the gentle morning light, he could see the features of the Endarian princess who had graced his life with her love. Her auburn hair and mocha skin were several shades lighter than those of her people, but her facial features were just as refined as those of her mother, Queen Elan. At six feet, she was taller than John but a head shorter than most Endarians.

Princess Kimber had married John in Endar Pass in a ceremony conducted by the queen herself. Elan had then set them on the quest that had brought them here, to the mountain home of Kim's human father, High Lord Rafel. Together with their friends Arn and the Kanjari horse warrior Ty they had journeyed south to warn Carol of her part in the prophecy contained within the ancient *Scroll of Landrel*.

A shudder passed through Kim's body, and a low moan, almost a wail, escaped her lips. Sliding his arm around his beloved, John nestled against her, sudden concern filtering into his thoughts. He considered waking her but decided on the gentle comfort of holding her close to let the bad dream subside. The harsh images that painted themselves in his wife's sleep should not be her last experience before waking.

—⚬⚬—

Kimber strolled through the forest two leagues southeast of the white bridge that led to the Endarian Palace in Lake Endar's center. To her fourteen-year-old nose, the scent of pine and blue spruce gave her a sense of oneness with the ancient woods. Having completed her life-shifting training early, she had the afternoon off. So she had donned the color-shifting uniform that blended with whatever background she passed.

As she moved effortlessly through the woods, her thoughts returned to her training. Although the skills were rare, some Endarians possessed the talent for one of the two exchange magics, time-shaping or life-shifting. While Kimber's brother, Galad, possessed the time-shaping ability, Kimber was a life-shifter, though there were those who called it life-stealing. Her ability and her ongoing training in the use of her talent allowed her to form a channel that could transfer the life essence from one thing to another, healing an entity by hurting another.

Although certain Endarian sects used this ability in combat, the law forbade the practice of intentionally harming an intelligent being to heal another. So the life-shifters funneled energy from plants into those they sought to heal, although this was far more difficult to do since the life essences were so different.

Like time-shaping, life-shifting magic also had its cost. To create a channel, Kim could start funneling her own essence into those she wanted to heal. Thus, injuries corresponding to what she healed formed on her body. If she could maintain concentration, she could complete

11

the channel, drawing life essence into herself from the nearby plants, repairing her body while flora perished. It was as sad as it was painful. And if Kim lost her focus, she could die from the wounds accepted.

A movement in the bushes brought Kimber's head around. She whistled and was rewarded by a happy yelp as a large golden-haired beast bounded from the nearby thicket. Kimber knelt to wrap her arms around the dog, laughing as its long tongue licked her face.

"Leala," she said, "I've missed you, too. Show me those pups of yours."

But as she rose to follow the dog back into the thicket, a familiar voice brought her to a stop. "Hello, Kimber."

She spun to see Erelis, an older Endarian boy who had asked the queen for permission to court her. Despite Kimber's objections, Elan had given Erelis her permission. Kimber knew why. Erelis was the scholar that Elan wished her son, Galad, was, and the queen was thus blind to the suitor's shortcomings. Despite his handsome face, something about Erelis greatly repelled Kimber, and yesterday she had made that fact plain to him.

"You followed me!" she said, letting fury fill her voice.

Erelis stepped forward, surprising her when he grabbed her hand and pulled her into an embrace. She tried to pull away, but he was stronger; his breath came in ragged pants. He tripped her and fell to the ground atop her body, pinning Kimber. She tried to strike out at him but could not free a hand to do so. His face lowered toward hers, and she turned her head away. It didn't matter. She felt his hot breath and lips on her throat and screamed, her mind reeling with disbelief that this was happening. But this far into the woods, there was no one to hear her cries.

But then Leala was on Erelis, snarling as she grabbed his leg and pulled. With a curse, Erelis released Kimber and kicked at the dog. When Leala did not let go, Erelis grabbed a thick stick and struck the dog in the face, sending her tumbling away. His face contorted in fury, he rose to his feet, putting all his strength into a blow that put out an eye and dropped Leala to the ground, bleeding from the mouth.

"No!" Kimber screamed as Erelis raised the stick to deliver another blow.

Fury misted Kimber's eyesight as she called upon her life-shifting talent, knowing that what she was about to do was forbidden. Forming the channel, she funneled her own health into the dog, accepting Leala's agony as terrible wounds formed on Kimber's body. Her consciousness tried to fade, but she would not allow that to happen. Instead, Kimber completed the channel, extracting the life essence that she required from Erelis.

She ignored his screams. His actions had revealed the ugliness that rotted his soul. The shifting cycle continued until both she and Leala were made whole once again.

Erelis collapsed to the ground, his hands clutching at his crushed eye. His shattered jaw tried to form words but merely managed a mewling sound. For several moments, Kimber stared down at what she had done. Then she turned her back on the grisly sight and ran.

—⁂—

Kim sat up so rapidly that John leapt from the bed, his eyes casting about for danger. She was shivering badly, unable to stop the tremors that cascaded through her body. The dream had resurrected the horrible memory that she had worked so hard to repress. She hadn't just hurt Erelis. She had known at a glance that the wounds he had inflicted on the dog would be fatal. Yet she had not hesitated to transfer them to Erelis, and his body was unable to cope with the trauma. To save a dog, she had killed one of her own people. Even worse, she knew that, given the same circumstances, she would do it again.

The Endarian High Council had called Princess Kimber before a committee of inquisition. Although they had eventually found her actions justified, she had sworn that she would never again take life essence from animals or any higher beings. It was a promise she had kept since that day.

John sat beside her, taking her gently in his arms. "What is it, Kim? What is wrong?"

Unable to speak, she dropped her head to her husband's shoulder and wept.

4

Great Forest
YOR 414, Late Winter

Alan struggled to open his eyes. Had someone stuck his eyelids closed with sap? As he managed the task, a familiar face swam into his field of vision. He tried to sit up and then sank back with a gasp. He was as weak as a newborn kitten, probably weaker. At least a kitten could move around.

A firm hand pressed him back to the blankets that lay spread on the ground.

"Easy now, Alan." Derek Scot's voice worked its way into Alan's head.

Alan's tongue moved over lips that felt odd. The taste in his mouth was nasty, and he could only imagine how his breath smelled. Worse than tasting bad, it felt bad. His teeth seemed to have developed some kind of fungus, as had his tongue.

Something was missing. The itching. His left arm had been itching for what seemed like an eternity, and now that was gone. Gone? He twisted his head, trying to get a look at it.

"Relax," said Derek. "You still have your arm, although it's going to be tough getting it back into shape. That was good thinking, using the maggots like that, although I daresay you were lucky to find them this time of year. You must have been pretty far out to be that low in altitude."

Suddenly it all came rushing back to Alan. "Greg. Kelly. I tried to bring them back, but I don't know . . ."

Derek nodded. "It's all right. You and Ty still had their bodies when we found you. You had made it all the way to the west edge of the Great Forest. You were burning up with fever and delirious. To tell you the truth, we thought we might lose you before we could get you back to our main camp. We would have, too, if it hadn't been for the maggots on that wound. Now, I'll bet you're hungry."

"Hungry?" Alan searched his feelings, gradually achieving an awareness of the gnawing at the pit of his stomach.

"We'll prepare some hearty mushroom soup. My guess is that you won't be able to handle much more than that considering how long you've been out."

"Look, Derek," said Alan, "I need to tell you about what happened."

"Yes, and I want to hear it," said Derek. "But first we're going to get some food and hot tea into your body. You've been in and out of consciousness for three weeks. We had to force some broth down your throat that whole time. I daresay you've lost a few pounds."

Alan raised his head, although it felt like lifting a massive stone. As he looked at the skinny body stretched out on the blankets, he marveled that it was his. Derek reached around behind him, dragging a pack into position to lean back against. The relief Alan felt in letting himself sink back was profound. As if it was surprised to see him awake, Derek's large black bear cub, Lonesome, crowded in to sniff Alan. But at Derek's command of "Away," Lonesome ambled off.

Alan took a shaky breath. How had he come to this? For most of his twenty years, Alan had dreamed of becoming a great leader like his father, the legendary high lord who had led the army of Tal to victory in the Vorg War. Throughout the years of his training, Alan had gone undefeated in contests of arms, beating lads several years his senior. But he had become a disappointment to his father, who had sent him out with the rangers, hoping that Derek Scot could teach Alan the sense of responsibility required of a leader. Instead, on his first long-range patrol, Alan had been responsible for the deaths of both rangers whom he commanded. Once again, he had been rash, giving in to battle lust when he should have focused upon those he was supposed to lead.

His head swimming with memories, he let depression drag him into bloody dreams.

—⁓—

Through the coming days, Alan drove himself relentlessly to regain his strength. When he wasn't exercising his body, he ate or slept. At first, he found that he could barely lift his left arm, so he concentrated on that, forcing himself to lift his sword above his head and back down.

Over the weeks that followed, he graduated to his ax. He also started going on long walks through the woods. Ty often accompanied him when he wasn't out on patrol. During those walks, the blond Kanjari horse warrior taught him fine points of wielding his ax that had escaped Alan's military trainers.

He learned stances that flowed from one to the next, adding speed, precision, and power to each blow. Ty taught him variations of these movements that could be performed from horseback. And Alan paid attention. As annoying as he had once thought the Kanjari's wit, he now took no offense at Ty's gibes. They often masked a deeper meaning intended to increase the lord's understanding of the skills he practiced. And it seemed to Alan that his efforts even impressed the towering barbarian.

Alan's strength improved to the point that he began chopping wood from fallen logs, using a wood ax first with his left hand, then with his right hand, back and forth. Before long he was wielding an ax in each hand, alternating strokes, driving himself through longer and longer sessions. Even the rangers marveled at the way the lord drove himself.

Running through the woods replaced walking. Soon he added a full pack to his back on his long runs, finally running in full chain mail with weapons. An exercise Alan grew to love was tree climbing, something that in the Great Forest was an awe-inspiring activity. The giant trees grew upward for hundreds of feet.

Since the trunks were so wide, the way into the treetops was accomplished by grabbing handholds in the rough bark and scrambling up as you would on a rock wall. The world changed in the upper reaches of the forest. The limbs were blanketed in snow and were quite slick. This added greatly to the challenge of the climb since Alan had to maintain a grip with one hand and his feet while clearing snow away from his next handhold with the other hand.

The sights took Alan's breath away. The great trees stretched away on all sides, draped in snow deep enough to cause the thinner limbs up high to bend downward under the weight. On sunny days, the brightness reflected from the snowy boughs was dazzling, scattering a multitude of colors from icicles clinging to the branches.

As the days wore on and his strength returned, Alan continually asked Derek to put him back on patrol duty with the other rangers. With winter's advance, Derek finally agreed that he was ready. Since Alan's mistakes had gotten rangers killed, he was immensely relieved to be given another chance. He vowed to the gods that he would never tow another packtrain of dead men back to camp.

5

The ranger patrols began spotting increased signs of military activity in the low country. The rise in the number of vorgish and human scouts wasn't a good sign. The army of the protectors had apparently established a camp in the low foothills, where it awaited the thaws of spring before moving toward Areana's Vale.

The question was, where was the main camp? To find out, Derek wanted to extend the range of the patrols. Due to the danger of working their way through the increasing numbers of vorgish scouts, Derek decided to send a six-man patrol instead of the usual three. That left him with ten rangers and Ty to continue scouting the area closer to Areana's Vale.

George Dalton led a group consisting of Harry Budka, Jim Clemens, Sam Jacobson, Bill Harrison, and Alan. Alan was the youngest of the bunch but had seen more combat than Bill, who had just qualified as a ranger the past summer.

As they finished preparing their packs, George briefed the team. Their mission was to find the army of the protectors and get an estimate of the horde's size to see if it matched with what Blade had reported. If it did, then another group had likely not split off to attack from a different location. George doubted that such tactics would make sense owing to the funneling effect of the canyon leading into the vale, but it was still best to know exactly how many soldiers Rafel would be facing.

They were to try to avoid becoming engaged with the enemy. Alan thought that George stared directly at him while making this point, although it could have been his imagination. George then directed Alan to ride with him in the pairings.

Saddling their horses, the team moved out, making their way directly toward the location where Alan had encountered the vorg patrol. Subsequent ranger patrols had also identified vorgish activity in the area.

Two scouts rode well out on the flanks and another pair far forward, with Alan positioned a few paces off to the side of George. The ranger apparently didn't want to take any chances that Alan would get them caught up in a fight when they were on a reconnaissance mission. The perceived slight chafed at Alan, but there was little he could do except stay quiet and alert.

Having moved swiftly down out of the higher mountains, within four days the rangers reached the point where the battle had taken place. The outriders had picked up nothing to cause concern. Talk was not something that George specialized in, and it would have been inappropriate during the patrol. Still, the silence weighed heavily upon Alan, as if the others were judging his every move. Several times he caught one of the other rangers staring in his direction, or perhaps they were only looking back toward George.

The countryside dropped off rapidly, each set of rolling hills lower than the last. The air was much warmer down at this elevation, the daytime temperatures rising well above freezing. In George's determination to stay within the wooded areas, the pace slowed. Finally the group reached a point where the hills became nearly bare of trees and were separated by broad and grassy valleys. Winter's effects had turned the hills and valleys to light brown.

They now began traveling only at night, holing up during the day in thickets or in stands of trees where no one could observe them. George turned northward, paralleling the open valley land that lay just to the west, keeping to the best cover available. Although the riders saw signs of passage, they did not see any movement of enemy troops until they were seven days into the patrol.

The day was hazy and cool, and they were operating from a hidden position on a small hill from which they could look out across the great valley. A low warbling whistle from Bill, who was posted on northern watch, alerted them that he had spotted something. Then the south watch issued a warning.

George signaled for the rangers to move up, and they crawled into positions along the leading edge of brush. From his location, Alan spotted three separate groups of riders, two of which rode werebeasts and the third group was on horseback. Altogether he counted sixty-five riders. They were not traveling together, but all were headed south along the line of hills in which the rangers now hid. Alan estimated that the closest group was still at least a league away and would pass well below the rangers' position if the riders kept to their current course.

George signaled for the rangers to fall back to their rally position deeper in the wood line. As soon as all had arrived, he quickly reviewed the situation as seen from each position. Satisfied, George ordered the rangers to move quietly eastward, putting distance between themselves and the large patrols.

Leading their horses and mounting once they were far enough away to avoid being seen or heard, the rangers moved farther back into the foothills and turned north again, bypassing the forward cavalry elements they had seen riding to the south. They continued moving carefully northward until darkness had fallen. Then, once again, George turned them back toward the west.

Shortly after midnight, the rangers spotted specks of flame. The army encampment was far out in the plain and dotted with hundreds of campfires, spreading for leagues in all directions. Beyond that, Alan could tell nothing about the layout of the army that occupied the camp.

"We'll set up an observation position here in the wood line," said George. "I want to watch that camp in daylight, put together a detailed assessment of everything we see, and then sneak out of here tomorrow night. Sam and Bill, set up about a hundred paces off to the right.

"Harry, you and Jim take the horses to the little creek we passed a quarter league back and stake them out near the water. Then return immediately and pick out an observation position a hundred paces down on the left. Alan and I will pick a spot in the center. Wait until it's good and dark tomorrow night to move, and then we'll meet back here and go get the horses."

Toward dawn, a cold drizzle began falling; it threatened to change to freezing rain as the gray of morning came. The change in the weather reduced visibility to the point that daylight did not improve the rangers' ability to see the camp. To the contrary, they could now barely make out the outlines of the near edge, some two leagues away from their position.

By noon, the threatened freezing rain had begun in earnest, soaking them where they lay and crusting them over with a thin sheet of ice. Alan flexed his aching arms and legs in a near continuous repetition as he fought to keep still but retain enough body heat to avoid a severe case of chills. The rangers were all doing their own variations of exercise-in-place to stay warm.

When they gathered at the selected spot that night, George gave the expected order that they would remain in place for another day and hope for better conditions. Everyone resumed their positions.

"Alan, I want you to go back and check on the horses," George said. "If you need to, move them to a different spot where they can get to some fresh grass, but keep them hidden. Then get back here before dawn."

"On my way."

Alan felt glad to move, covering the half league over the hill and back into the small canyon to the west with long strides, stopping periodically to listen just in case something besides him was moving in the darkness.

When he first arrived at the secluded spot where they had staked the horses, he thought that they had broken free and wandered off. Then he heard a soft nickering and saw movement under the trees to his left. The horses were all there but standing close together under the shelter of the branches. He bent down and felt the ground. As he had suspected, the horses had finished off the grass in the area and would need to be moved.

Leaving them where they were, he scouted the area for another spot, finding one with just enough grass another quarter of a league upstream to the northeast. The area was small, with access to the stream and surrounded by trees. By the time he had gotten the horses to their new grazing spot and had staked them out once more, the gray tinges of dawn were beginning to show on the eastern horizon.

Satisfied, he turned and moved swiftly back toward the spot where the rangers lay watching. Whether it was a distant noise or catching sight of movement that brought him to a stop, Alan wasn't sure. He sank low in the brush, watching and listening. The sound of heavy breathing and moving feet directed his attention off to his left. A group of vorgs on foot were moving along the streambed. In the dim light he counted fifteen, but there may have been more. Alan slipped back into the deeper brush, moving as quickly and as quietly as he could toward the rangers.

As he reached the camp, he stepped up beside the waiting George. "We've got trouble."

George listened as Alan described the situation. The vorgs were almost certainly going to pass through the spot where the rangers had originally staked the horses, and when the vorgs got there, they would pick up Alan's scent.

George wasted no time calling the rangers in and briefing them.

"We have to move quickly now. Stay together. If the vorgs keep moving in the direction Alan saw them moving in, then we should be able to get in front of them by heading directly for the spot we first staked out the horses. We'll stop in that bunch of trees up the hill a hundred feet on this side of the stream and wait for them. Nobody is to shoot until I give the signal. Let's go."

The rangers swept silently over the backside of the hill and down into the trees below. The light of dawn now made the vorgs visible as they came up the streambed only two hundred paces downstream. Suddenly one of the lead vorgs picked up a scent and rushed forward. He snarled loudly, and another eighteen vorgs joined him, tramping over the spot, sniffing the air, looking for the horses' trail.

George raised his bow, the bows of the rangers and Alan echoing his movement. He stood and fired, and six arrows flew simultaneously down into the vorgs below, five of whom fell to the ground, one with two arrows sticking from its chest.

As the first vorgs collapsed, their comrades turned to meet the attack, racing across the ground separating them from the rangers. A second volley landed upon the charging vorgs, and three more rolled onto the ground.

Alan rose with his ax as the rangers pulled their swords and rushed to meet the leading warriors. A great she-vorg rushed at Alan, and he split her head helmet to chin, whirling to meet the attack of a second and a third. Other vorgs assailed the rangers, maces, flails, and scimitars rising and falling as metal clashed against metal.

A second vorg went down before the fury of Alan's whirling ax, the force of the blow lifting the vorg from his feet and slamming him into a vorg that fought with Bill, the three bodies going down in a pile. Bill thrust upward with his short sword, spilling the guts of the warrior on top of him.

"Left flank," Alan yelled, pointing at a vorg that raced away up the canyon at a dead run.

"Get him," yelled George, who battled two others.

Alan's legs stretched out as he ran across the hill. The vorg had the lead and was fast, but Alan was faster. The distance between them gradually closed. The vorg crested the hill, heading directly down it toward the camp in the flat beyond. Alan redoubled his effort, forcing every bit of strength and speed out of his body. His lungs were a blacksmith's bellows, gulping air. He was within ten paces, then five paces.

Reaching striking distance, Alan whirled his ax, hammering it down into the middle of the vorg's back. The warrior tumbled to the ground, attempting to rise but driven down for the last time by the force of a follow-up blow.

Alan looked out at the camp now only a league away from him, a gasp escaping his lips. Thousands of tents stretched out as far as he could see. Columns of smoke rose from hundreds of fires to create a pall. Even at this distance, the acrid smell burned Alan's nose. And everywhere that he looked, vorgs and men moved through the encampment. He made a quick estimate of the number of troops in a section and then estimated the number of sections of camp the size he had just counted. Then he turned and sprinted back toward the fight.

Alan arrived at the location of the rangers to find all the vorgs dead. George and Bill knelt beside Jim, bandaging a wound on his thigh as Sam stood watch over them.

"Harry?" Alan asked.

Sam shook his head sadly. "Harry didn't make it."

"How is Jim?"

"He caught a knife through the thigh, but I think he'll live."

Alan looked around. The vorg bodies lay strewn across the ground. Of the group of rangers, Alan was the only one who was unhurt. Except for Jim, their injuries were minor.

George finished bandaging Jim and walked over to Alan. "I take it you got the one you were chasing?"

Alan summarized the chase and what he had seen of the camp from where he had caught the runner.

"That was standout work on your part today," George said.

"Sure was," added Sam.

"You did everything just fine," said George. "You kept a clear head and got the information I needed about the war camp. You've seen me keeping an eye on you. Based upon what I've seen out here, you can ride with me any day."

Murmurs of agreement came from the other rangers.

"Thank you," said Alan, working to keep the tremor he felt from his voice.

"Alan, carry Jim back to his horse," said George. "I've got Harry. Since we have the information we came for, let's get out of here before someone misses the patrol we just ended."

6

Endar Pass
YOR 414, Late Winter

Queen Elan watched as her son stared back at her, defiance shining brightly in his dark eyes. She understood why her proposal angered Galad so. In battle, his long black hair swirled around him as he fought. He became a fearsome vision of death. Being the leader of an elite brigade of fifteen hundred time-mist warriors was what he wanted from this world.

The mist warriors fought within the murky tendrils of fog that their time-shapers sent forth to disrupt and confuse attacking armies. Operating in the mists was a difficult skill to acquire, and being such a warrior had its costs. Fighting within the fogs of time posed tremendous challenges since a person could only see or interact with another when time moved at the same pace for both parties. It was easy to become disoriented within the mists, moving from a tactically advantageous region into one where you were at a disadvantage—one of the reasons so few elite mist warriors existed.

The time-mists were of two types, rychly and pomaly, two ancient terms from the long-gone era of Landrel. The passage of time slowed within the pomaly mists and accelerated in the rychly mists, balancing each other. Passing from a slower mist into one within which time passed faster was like fighting your way out of thick mud. The reverse was true as one exited a rychly mist, stepping into a slower zone, pressing oneself into mud instead of out of it. If the time difference between mists was too great, passage between them became impossible. Thus, any time-shaper who supported mist warriors created complicated flows that contained relatively gentle gradients. Learning to recognize those gradients took long to master. And because the time-mist warriors preferred to traverse the rychly mists, where time passed more quickly, they aged at an accelerated rate . . . another reason for the scarcity of special warriors.

Despite Galad's blatant scorn, still the queen pressed him.

"The reason I forced you to spend your youth learning the art of time-shaping is because our elders recognized a talent within you unmatched among our people. You have a duty to use your ability to channel those mists."

"My sense for their ebb and flow allows me to lead mist warriors as no other can."

The queen stepped forward to place a hand on his sword arm, her turquoise gown swirling about her slender form in the gentle breeze. At six and a half feet, she could look him squarely in the eyes. Galad's uniform shifted colors to match the forest behind him, highlighting his face. They stood facing each other atop the white bridge that spanned the gap between the city walls and the turquoise lake's south shore.

"Ever petulant, Galad. Why must you argue with me about this?" she asked. "You can do far more good for your brigade as a time-shaper than you can as its commander."

"Laikas fills that role in my command. She has great talent."

"Only the skills that she has developed through practice make her your superior," said Elan as tension built in her back. "You know how rare the time-shaping talent is. Its scarcity prohibits me from assigning more than one time-shaper to each brigade. My scouts have reported that Kragan's army nears the foothills a hundred leagues to the southeast of Endar. Step aside. Give your command to your deputy so that you may fulfill the role our people so desperately need in the coming fight."

"That I will not do, though it pains me to ignore your command. As good as Captain Tempas is, she cannot read the mists as I do. Even Laikas cannot manage that. It is impossible to see what passes within one mist while occupying another, but I can sense the subtle variations in those fogs. Those differences build images in my mind that become visions of how my enemies move. No, Mother, my destiny is to fight in the mists, not to summon them."

Galad stepped back, shrugging off Elan's imploring hand, filling her with frustration. His slight bow did nothing to alleviate the feeling.

"My command awaits me, my queen. I shall do as I have always done and lead my mist warriors to victory in your service. Now . . . by your leave, I must go."

Elan stood alone on the bridge, watching her son jog off to join the brigade of mist warriors, men and women, who awaited him in the woods. As he disappeared into the trees, the setting sun bathed the snowcapped southeastern peaks in blood.

7

The rangers traveled single file up the creek, seeking to lose their scent in its waters. For two leagues, the stream continued to wind to the northeast, never very wide and only a foot or so deep. At last they reached a point where it emerged from a spring in the floor of the shallow canyon. Having lost their ability to mask their trail, George ordered the rangers to move to an outrider formation and turned to climb directly east toward the mountains. They crossed over ridgelines and then up steep little draws, intending to get back to deep cover as quickly as possible. Once in the heavy woods, they would head south, turning back to the east only when they were on a line that would take them to the Great Forest.

That night, the rangers paused for a brief rest and then began moving once again, single file in the darkness to avoid becoming separated. Toward dawn, they reached another small stream and again turned to follow its course, wading upstream through the running water. After several leagues, George again turned them toward the high mountains in the east.

A shrill whistle split the air. Alan looked up to see Sam, the southern outrider, coming back toward them at a dead run. On his heels, seven horsemen raced after him, curved swords drawn. George pointed back to the west, where another group of thirty men had crested the hill a half league behind them and were now coming hard.

"Find defensible terrain, now!" George yelled.

The rangers brought their horses to a run, although the animal carrying Harry's body slowed the group. As they entered the wood line, George signaled, and his men spun to face the direction from which Sam had been running. His horse raced into the trees past the spot where his fellow rangers waited, bows at the ready. Within seconds the small group of riders who had been chasing Sam came into view, and the waiting group of rangers released a volley of arrows, unhorsing all but three of the attackers, who immediately struggled to turn their horses back. A second volley of arrows ended their efforts.

Once again George whirled his horse around, leading the rangers up the hills to the east, where Bill and Sam, the two outriders, joined them. The entire group now rode together, still towing the horse carrying Harry. Alan noted that the wound on Jim's leg had begun bleeding heavily again, as evidenced by the blood dripping from his boot and the deathly paleness of his face. If they didn't get to a place where they could bandage it soon, Jim could bleed to death. If they stopped now, they would probably all bleed out.

The riders chasing them broke from the wood line the rangers had left just a minute before, gaining ground steadily. Some of the riders were well out in front of the others, lying low across their horses' necks, hoping to be the first to catch the rangers.

Alan searched the hillsides to their front, but he could see nothing that would give them a significant advantage. George continued to press forward, topping the ridge and then swinging along it, dropping to the military crest on the far side. Alan guessed that they were no more than forty seconds ahead of the lead riders whom he could no longer see, masked as they were by the reverse slope of the hill.

Suddenly Jim yelled out, "Do not stop! I'll delay them a few seconds."

His horse spun sideways and into a thicket.

George waved them on. Alan understood the decision, but a cold anger burned within him. How many more of his friends did he have to watch die? Still, he stayed with the main group.

Behind them two riders raced over the ridgeline, only to tumble into the dirt as Jim worked his bow. Five more crested the rise, and again two of them fell before the other three plowed into the thicket where Jim waited. The main group of marauders rushed past, once again closing ground on the remaining rangers.

Reluctantly, George released the lead rope of the horse that carried Harry's corpse and increased speed. There were four of them now— George, Sam, Bill, and Alan—riding with reckless abandon up and down shale-covered slopes where most men would dismount to lead their horses on foot. Alan was worried about the animals. They were running at the brink of exhaustion and would die under their riders if pushed much farther. Suddenly George spotted something, spurring his horse up a steep slope, then jumping off to disappear into a narrow gap in the walls of a cliff. The others did the same, smacking their horses' rumps to send them running away.

The crevice was only wide enough for one man at a time to walk through and led up and back toward the crest of the hill.

"Bill, Sam," yelled George. "Get up and block the high end. Don't let any of them get past you. Alan and I will hold from here."

Without a word, the other two rangers ran up the narrow trail. Almost as soon as they had disappeared, the sound of horses scrambling up the slope and the yells of dismounting warriors filled Alan's ears. He hefted his ax and waited. George stood just below him on the trail, the first to block the path.

Alan leaned forward. "Let me by you. You can work a bow better than I, but I'm better with an ax or sword."

George shook his head. "Not today, son."

Frustrated, but seeing no way that he could wield the ax around George, Alan set it aside and took up his bow.

A yell preceded the first of the marauders into the gap in front of them, and Alan put an arrow into his chest. As the man staggered forward, George cut his throat. Another clambered over the top of his comrade's body, his sword deflecting George's stroke as the clash of metal rang between the chasm walls. Alan struggled to get in position to fire past the ranger, but repeatedly George blocked his view. George thrust, and his opponent fell, again replaced by another.

Alan managed a shot, striking the fellow in the right shoulder. The brigand howled, shoving his shield ahead, sending George's blow glancing off. He surged forward, pushed by those behind him, the force of their thrust upon the shield sending George sprawling backward.

Alan filled the gap, grabbing his ax as he stepped over George. The raiders tried their previous tactic, shoving violently forward with the shield. This time, Alan met the attack with the full force of his weight upon his ax, splitting the shield and embedding it in the man who held it. He kicked the dying body, sending it back into the bandit who followed.

Advancing, Alan used his ax to behead the marauder who struggled to disengage himself from the corpse. Two arrows whisked by Alan's ear as George worked his bow, and another man fell. Alan shoved his way over the corpses in front of him, yelling wildly as he closed with the next man in line. The anger he had been holding inside burst its bonds, immersing him in a white-hot rage that left no room for thought.

The great ax rose and fell, rose and fell, as arrows whistled across his shoulder. And before him, raiders died, only to be replaced by others. The rocks dripped red on both sides of the narrow chasm. Suddenly the rush below them paused as the men who waited outside became reluctant to enter the killing ground.

A yell from above caused Alan to look back. On the high side of the chasm, Bill struggled mightily but was being pushed back down the path toward them, Sam apparently having fallen earlier.

George waved Alan back. "Go help young Bill. I'll hold this end."

Alan raced up the path, reaching Bill just as he staggered, a sword slashing his side. Alan grabbed his shoulder, tossing Bill behind him as he swung his ax with the other hand. The blow only partially connected with the sword that sought to block it, but its force was enough to break the blade. The bandit stabbed with the broken shard, but Alan smashed the blunt trailing edge of his ax into the man's face, caving it in and sending him flying limply backward.

The upper part of the enemy force wavered under the onslaught as Alan worked his way up the path. He split the skull of the next man in line, impatiently tossing his body aside so that he could step forward to greet the next. His ax handle grew slick with blood.

A sword sliced Alan's cheek open, but he paid no notice, his whirling ax severing the arm that held it, continuing in its great arc to remove the head from the body to which the limb had been attached. A low moan arose from those who stood before him. Trapped by those behind, they could not retreat before the blood-covered demon whose ax swept them from this world into the next.

Alan's muscles bulged with exertion, and his breath now came in mighty gulps, but still he pushed forward. As he reached the upper entrance to the chasm, the last two men turned and ran toward their horses. Two arrows whispered over his shoulder, catching the first as he tried to mount and sending the second tumbling from his horse.

Alan glanced back to see Bill, weak with blood loss, lowering his bow and dropping to one knee, a knee that slowly gave way beneath him. Alan grabbed the ranger in one arm and carried him back down the chasm toward where he had left George. The old veteran sat at the lower entrance to the cavern among the corpses, a lone arrow jutting from his upper chest. He raised his head to look at Alan, who set Bill gently against the wall next to George.

Seeing the question in Alan's eyes, George spat a red wad from his mouth and said, "I nailed the last one to a tree down there as he let loose this shaft. I was just a hair slow."

The ranger chuckled softly, a sound that took on a gurgle toward the end. He spat another wad of red phlegm against the wall.

"Ah, George," Alan said, a sudden wave of exhaustion and sadness assailing him.

"Don't you die on us now," said Bill, himself pale from blood loss.

"Too late, son," said George.

Then he turned his head toward Alan, and a broad grin split his face.

"I'm just glad I got to see this day, glad I got a chance to be a part of it. Alan, I swear to the gods I have never seen the like of what you did here. Your father would burst with pride. I wish I was going to be around to tell him, to see his face."

With one last effort, the veteran thrust out his arm, catching Alan's wrist in a strong grip. "You get Bill on back safely, okay?"

"I will, boss. You have my word on it."

The ranger smiled one last time and sank back against the wall, dead.

Alan stood and screamed his frustration to the wind, a wild, lonely sound that echoed away into the canyons beyond.

8

Endless Valley
YOR 414, Late Winter

Bill's gasp brought Alan back to reality. He stripped away the ranger's shirt and examined the wound, which was shallow but bleeding heavily. Alan bandaged it, holding pressure against the injury with his hand until the blood flow stopped. He would have to check the wound frequently during travel to ensure that the bleeding did not resume.

Alan had endured similar wounds and had experience treating others that were far worse. Travel complicated the matter considerably. He picked up the semiconscious ranger and carried him out of the narrow chasm, working his way along the hillside toward a place that provided adequate cover. A dense and thorny manzanita thicket worked.

Having made Bill as comfortable as possible, Alan began looking for the horses. He found them, along with several of the mounts that the marauders had ridden, grazing on the scant grass at the bottom of the draw. The afternoon sun glinted off the water of a beaver pond. He worked quickly, gathering up his horse and five others. Retrieving waterskins from several of the packs, he filled these in the stream and tied them to saddles.

He led the packtrain back up to the entrance of the narrow chasm. By the time he had retrieved the bodies of his fellow rangers from among the piles of the dead, the light of day was waning. Alan tied the bodies of his friends across the saddles, his breathing coming in ragged gasps unrelated to the effort involved. Then he swung his leg over his mount and headed back to where he had left Bill.

He felt crusty, the blood that drenched him—some his, some from others—having long since begun to dry. The cut on his face, which began just above his left eyebrow and passed down his left cheek, still wept a congealing red ooze. The cheek had not quite opened all the way through except in a half-inch tear in the center. Even that had closed with the clotting of the blood. Depression assailed him, making him long to lie down next to Bill and sleep, hoping that he would awake to find he had merely been having a very bad nightmare.

That was not to be. Alan still had to backtrack and find the bodies of his other two comrades. Harry had been tied to a horse when they had been forced to release it, and Jim had fallen trying to slow their attackers during their mad dash to the chasm. Alan would not leave them to rot, their bones forgotten in the land of enemies.

Bill roused as Alan examined his wounds in preparation for travel. He grimaced but made no sound.

"Drink some water," said Alan, tipping the flask to Bill's lips.

The ranger drank thirstily and struggled to a sitting position.

"You look like the deep," he said, staring at Alan's face.

"Yeah, well, you've looked better yourself."

As Bill's gaze took in the horses, with their dead comrades draped across their saddles, an expression as grim as Alan's mood settled over his youthful face, a face that looked as if it had aged several years in a day.

"Harry and Jim?" Bill asked.

"As soon as we can get you mounted, we're going back to find them. We should be able to find Jim tonight, but Harry is tied to his horse. We'll have to track him in the morning."

"Let's get going then," said Bill, grimacing in pain as he got to his feet, his face pallid in the gathering twilight.

"I want you to tell me immediately if that wound opens up again," Alan said. "If you try to gut it out and keep it to yourself, you'll just hurt us both. If you notice it has opened, let me know. I'm going to need your help on this trip. If you pass out from unnecessary blood loss, that won't happen."

"I'll pay attention."

"Good."

Alan helped the injured ranger onto his horse, noting that he managed to sit well enough once mounted.

The riders made their way slowly and carefully back to where Jim had died, keeping well away from the path they had taken on their initial ride in case other marauders had discovered that trail. They found Jim's body just after midnight, full of so many arrows that it looked like a spiny monster in the pale glow of the quarter moon. Alan snapped off the shafts before lifting Jim's corpse onto a horse and tying it firmly in place.

Alan then led Bill to a secluded spot where they dismounted to rest and wait for dawn. Sitting cross-legged, leaning back against the rough trunk of a juniper, Alan cast his glance toward the spot where Bill sat. In the fading darkness, the lad appeared to be a ghostly outline of himself, seeming to fade away as Alan tried to focus on him. A shudder of dread fluttered through Alan as he wondered momentarily if this was perhaps a portent of the young ranger's fate. The night was silent except for the faint rasp of Bill's breathing and the mutter of Alan's heartbeat. No gentle breeze stirred the boughs above his head or swept away the dampness of his condensed breath.

—⚬⚬⚬—

The cold light of the gray dawn found the two rangers and their pack-train of the dead working their way along the trail left by Harry's horse,

Alan following it easily except for rocky stretches that forced him to dismount to avoid losing the path. A dreary drizzle wept down upon the men, matching their mood. Alan was thankful that the threatened rain was slow in coming lest the trail be washed away, along with hopes of recovering Harry's corpse. The thought angered him. If Alan must return to camp after suffering such heavy losses, at least he would bring with him the shells of the men who had accompanied him.

Rounding a bend, they spotted Harry. The saddle, to which George had tied the corpse, had slid awkwardly off to the left side so that Harry seemed to lean against the big animal for support as it munched at a thick patch of grass. Alan dismounted and secured the lead rope of the horse. Moving around the side, he loosened the cinch and hefted the saddle and Harry's body back into place before securing it firmly once more. The smell that arose from the corpse clogged Alan's nose with a stench so thick that he could almost feel it on his skin, a thin mucous membrane engulfing him. That was the way of death, creeping in to rob you of the last simple dignity.

Alan tied the horse to the back of their packtrain before mounting and heading toward the distant mountains to the east.

For five days, the two rangers worked their way back toward the Great Forest, where Derek's ranger camp lay in wait, sticking to the thickest brush and taking detours along rushing streams to throw off anyone who might cross their trail and decide to follow it. Despite Alan's best efforts at cleaning and bandaging Bill's wound, the lad continued to weaken, picking up a deep cough and a fever that worsened as days passed. Luckily the wound did not become infected.

The mountains rose before them now, seemingly close enough to reach out and touch through the crystal clearness of the high-country air. Gleaming patches of snow lingered beneath the trees on the shady sides of the hills and in the shadows of the canyons. Pine had replaced juniper as the predominant species, their pungent needles indicating that home was near. The passage of the gruesome packtrain startled herds of deer, sending them bounding along the slopes in graceful leaps.

Alan now rode double behind Bill, supporting the delirious ranger in his saddle. He paused repeatedly to wet a bandanna and wrap it around Bill's head to siphon away some of the heat of his fever. Still, Alan could feel the warmth radiating from the young man.

The young lord heard the high whistle several seconds before its meaning registered through the deep haze of exhaustion that cloaked him. He pulled his horse to a halt, bringing the entire packtrain up short. Three riders broke from the wood line a quarter league above him to the northeast, sweeping down the slope at a dead run. Rangers. The mixture of relief and sadness that assaulted Alan at the sight brought a wetness to his eyes that he rubbed away with a dirty knuckle. He remembered what he had sworn to the gods he would never do. Once again, he was returning to his comrades bringing only dead in his wake. He glanced at Bill. At least one was still alive and, with proper care, would recover.

Alan leaned back in his saddle to await the arrival of the rangers who raced headlong toward him. The looks of horror on their faces as they slid to a halt beside the packtrain were quickly replaced with the stern demeanor that was the ranger norm. Through the red haze that shrouded his vision, he recognized Thad Spate, Frederick Jeals, and Keith Sampson, good hands all. What had he seen in their faces along with disbelief as they had dismounted? It seemed to Alan that a judgment had been made, the outcome less than favorable.

Thad reached him first and lifted Bill down. Laying the ranger out carefully on the ground, he rapidly stripped the bandages from his wound and set about cleaning it. Alan dismounted slowly, the weariness weighting his body like the iron chains that bound dangerous prisoners. Keith reached out to help him, but Alan shrugged away, leaning against his horse for support as he staggered before righting himself to stand on his own.

"Let me examine that wound on your face," Keith said. "It has a bad look to it."

"I'll be all right until we get back. Bill is the one who needs the attention."

"Bill's getting attention. Now shut up, sit down, and let me check that cut. Are you hurt anywhere else?"

"Nothing serious, including this cut on my face," Alan insisted, although he followed orders and sat down heavily.

As Keith poured water on a handkerchief and scrubbed roughly at Alan's face, breaking away the scabs from his sliced forehead and cheek, Alan could see Frederick moving down the line of packhorses, examining each dead ranger in turn.

The grimace that pinched Frederick's face gained deeper purchase with each inspection until the thin covering of skin cracked and tore. Deep fissures spread in a latticework across his head, peeling back the skin to expose the bone beneath, fissures that now wept a thick gray pus but no blood. To his horror, Alan saw that the gray matter that slithered from the cracks in Frederick's face was not pus at all.

Alan lunged to his feet, knocking Keith backward as he rushed toward Frederick, then tripped and fell to his knee before righting himself once again.

"What in the deep?" Keith said as he lost his footing and sat down hard on the ground.

Frederick whirled toward Alan, who reached out to grab him by the shoulders. Once again reality shifted. The shock of seeing Frederick staring, his face normal in every way except for the probing look that gouged at Alan, brought him to a sliding halt. Alan swayed.

"Your face," he began. "But I saw it . . ."

Keith's hand settled firmly on Alan's shoulder, turning him so that their eyes locked. "You saw what?"

Alan turned to look at Frederick, once more noting the disapproving glare but no sign of skin-splitting, brain-flowing madness.

"Just for a moment, I thought I saw . . . Forget it. I guess I'm just too tired to make any sense."

"Just sit down a minute," said Frederick, "while we get Bill and the train ready to travel."

"I haven't seen anyone following me, but it's possible."

"The scouts are out," said Frederick. "They'll work your back trail to make sure you didn't pick up any unwanted followers. Now let's move out."

If he had not been without sleep for a week, if he was not weighted down with an overwhelming sense of loss and remorse, and if his sense of responsibility for the deaths of the rangers had not been so great, Alan would have rendered a detailed report of the mission to the rangers, even though he would have to repeat it to Derek Scot upon arrival at base camp.

As it was, he waited, allowing the rangers who now escorted him to form their own impressions. To them, results mattered. Even though Alan had not led the patrol on the way out, he oversaw what remained. George Dalton, dead. Harry Budka, dead. Jim Clemens, dead. Sam Jacobson, dead. Only Bill Harrison remained alive, and he clung to life tenuously.

Alan had been out on two patrols on the expedition and had one survivor, besides himself, to show for it. The results were in. He had been weighed, measured, and, in the minds of the rangers, most glaringly found wanting.

9

High Lord Rafel paced along the ramparts of the lower fortress, accompanied by Battle Master Gaar. The preparations for the coming battle continued unabated, driven relentlessly by Hanibal. The young captain with the long red hair already seemed the perfect likeness to his father in his ability to effectively command men at any task, causing Gaar to burst with obvious pride, although he never mentioned any of his son's accomplishments to Rafel directly. Yet the high lord missed nothing, as evidenced by the rapid rate at which he had promoted Hanibal through the ranks.

However, despite Hanibal's leadership and the extended efforts of the thousands of citizens who populated Areana's Vale, they were clearly not ready to defend themselves against the hordes of brigands, vorgs, and worse that reports said now marched toward their mountains. Blade had bought them a winter of preparation. Now all they could do was pray that it would be enough.

Rafel's thoughts shifted to his last sight of his daughter. Blade, mounted on his black horse, had carried her unconscious body out of the lower fort on their journey deeper into the high country. She had looked so pale and vulnerable that Rafel had thought his heart would stop beating. But if anyone could save Carol from the trauma caused by her study of strange new magic, it was Blade, protected as he was by his enchanted knife, Slaken.

Rafel straightened his shoulders. Worries about Carol were too terrible to be allowed purchase in his head, at least during the long hours of the day, when others looked to him to set a strong example.

Carol's brother was a different matter. He worried about Alan because he could not avoid seeing him. Rafel was greatly pained to see how the soldiers shunned his only son. Alan had returned from the long ranger patrol scarred on the face and in his soul. He was a changed man, and his father was not sure he liked what he saw.

Alan had always driven himself to work harder than any of his peers, but a wild joy and enthusiasm for life had supplemented that determination. Since the return of the ill-fated patrol, Alan's drive had become a singular obsession. He worked maniacally, barely sleeping, doing all his assigned tasks and dedicating himself to long hours of extra practice with weaponry, especially his ax. He had taken on a harder edge that made his training partners nervous.

The reports from the field were that Alan had fought exceptionally well, coming through nearly impossible odds to return from each of his two patrols. Bill Harrison, the lone survivor of the last patrol, had corroborated those reports. The young ranger was now so devoted to Alan that he seemed to be his shadow. Still, there was no denying that almost everyone who had fought beside Alan had died. That did not sit well with the soldiers.

Then the rumors had started. People whispered that Alan's hero, Ty, was the earthly incarnation of the Dread Lord, a mighty warrior from Kalanthal, realm of the dead. These rumblings had started after Ty had battled more than a dozen vorgs to save one of the horse warriors from the fortress city of Val'Dep. Ty, who had been bathing in a stream, had strode naked into battle, wielding his crescent-bladed ax. When the fight had ended, only the Kanjari's eyes had peered out through the blood that clothed him.

The horse-warrior legend had it that the Dread Lord, whom these people called the Dar Khan, would one day return to this world cloaked only in blood to take mortal form. From among his followers, the Dar Khan would select one, the Chosen, who would remain in this world after he departed. The Chosen would be the most terrible of all, attracting to himself the mightiest group of warriors to ever stride this world. And those who served beside the Chosen would die in glorious combat to rise once again in Kalanthal. Only when the Dar Khan's appetite for new recruits was satisfied would the Chosen himself fall in battle and return to his master.

Complete rubbish.

What angered Rafel most was that almost the entire population of the vale had apparently bought into the rumor. The legend had spread like wildfire among the soldiers, and most shied away from Alan. Nevertheless, a few of the hardiest fighters seemed attracted to him because of those tales. Rafel shook his head as if to clear it of these thoughts and resumed his inspection of the defenses.

The feeling of wrongness came over him gradually at first but grew steadily. Gaar had noticed it, too, the grizzled warrior stopping in his tracks and looking around. A sudden hush fell over the fortress. Where there had been a standard cacophony of spring sounds a moment ago, suddenly not an animal or insect could be heard. Only the sound of the river rushing down the steep channel broke the silence. Even the soldiers fell silent as they, too, noticed the change.

Above the north rim of the gorge, where skies had just been clear, thick black clouds now crawled over the rim. A group of soldiers in the courtyard saw them and stopped to stare, several pointing up at the unusual formation. It looked like an unnatural soup boiling over the edges of a witch's cauldron, thick tendrils reaching down along the canyon walls as the entire mass crept over and down.

The air was suddenly thick with moisture. As the edge of the cloud crept down the cliff, strong bursts of electricity sent blue balls of energy scurrying among the rocks. Weblike lightning arced across to the opposite cliff wall, followed by tremendous volleys of thunder that shook the foundations of the fortress beneath them and threatened to break the eardrums of the stunned onlookers below.

The ominous cloud crept down the wall until it was a mere thirty paces above the fortress. It paused, thickened, and bulged outward, moving directly across to touch the southern canyon wall. A downdraft of cold air turned the breath of the soldiers below into puffs of silver mist, visible in the unnatural darkness due to the lightning that crawled overhead. Above the fortress, a hundred feet up, inky blackness boiled, spiderwebbed with electrical arcs.

Rafel's attention turned to a pair of riders rounding the bend in the canyon below. He immediately recognized Arn atop that ugly horse he favored, but it took him several seconds to identify Carol as the one who rode beside him. She wore trousers and boots, with a white blouse. Carol's hair swirled around her head in the wind. The clarity with which he could see her in the near darkness was startling. A preternatural glow surrounded her. She was breathtaking in every regard, from the proud tilt of her chin to the confident and defiant look in her eyes, which seemed to flash with echoes of the lightning churning in the clouds above.

His gaze shifted to Arn, clothed entirely in black, the man's demeanor an icy harbinger of death to any who might challenge them. As the pair came closer, the air grew so cold that all who awaited quivered. A wave of liquid fear accompanied the icy blast. Rafel felt the emotion and marveled at its magnificence, seeing that Gaar's eyes also lit with recognition. How much time had passed since Rafel had experienced the thrill of genuine fear? He felt young again.

The drawbridge crashed down of its own accord as the soldiers who manned the winch were tossed aside by unseen hands. Carol and Arn rode calmly across, passing along the streets of the fortress and out through the rear gate toward the forts that guarded the upper end of the ravine. As the two riders disappeared beyond the wall, the sky cleared as rapidly as it had clouded. Another sound provided accompaniment to the return of normalcy—the collective gasp of hundreds of startled soldiers.

A snort escaped from Gaar's lips. "If that doesn't bear all the trademarks of a Blade demonstration, I'm an old woman."

Rafel's smile matched Gaar's own. "Apparently, my daughter and future son-in-law have come up with a way for her to reintroduce herself to her people."

"Well, it has style, I'll give it that," Gaar said, turning to look at the broken winch. "It's a little hard on the fortifications, though."

PART II

Why can I not see the ultimate outcome when all else is so luminous in my mind's eye? Is it because fate has not made up its mind? Or does destiny rest in the rune-covered haft of the blade that Death wields? Everything will depend on the choices Death shall be forced to make.

—From the *Scroll of Landrel*

10

Areana's Vale
YOR 415, Early Spring

Back home within Areana's Vale, Alan swung the woodsman's ax in great arcs, each swing sending a chunk of timber flying from the three-foot-thick trunk of the mighty spruce. The sinews rippled across his formerly thick torso, glistening under a thin sheen of sweat as he worked. The men on rest break near him whispered among themselves. They had been toiling in shifts for more than eight hours, strong men all, and were exhausted, but not Alan, who had worked his ax since before sunrise without even pausing for lunch. If anything, he seemed to grow stronger as the day progressed, driving himself with a monstrous will that allowed him no reprieve from his labors.

Beside him, Bill struggled to match his efforts, although it appeared that the ranger might pass out at any moment. His breathing came in ragged gasps that rattled in his throat. Still, he did not quit.

Two days had passed since Arn had escorted Alan's sister back into the vale, and Alan could not get that first sight of her out of his mind. He had been working, just like today, and she had ridden by him clothed in black and white, shimmering like a goddess. He had been so awestruck that he had failed to run down the hill to greet her. She had not seen him and continued up the valley.

When he had finally managed to find her, she had hugged him with more strength than he remembered. Despite her shock at seeing the scar down the left side of his face, the reunion felt wonderful. Far from the failing creature who had fled the valley, she was her old self again. That was not quite right . . . she had grown into something more. What, he did not know. As for Arn, Alan had never seen him so happy, not that he gave any indication of his elation when in public.

A rider galloped into the clearing behind Alan, pulling his mount to a halt just short of the resting men.

"Lord Alan," he called.

Alan leaned the ax against the partially severed tree trunk and strode toward the rider.

"What is it, Bob?"

"High Lord Rafel sent me to get you. He wants to see you in his council chambers. He said to make haste."

"On my way," said Alan, grabbing his shirt from a branch and slipping it on. "If he doesn't mind the smell, then I don't."

The rider whirled his mount around and galloped back the way he came.

"You guys can finish cutting the tree," said Alan. "And if one of you could remember to pack that wood ax I brought up here and return it to the tool barn, I would appreciate it."

"I'll do it," said a panting Bill.

Alan clapped his hand on the ranger's shoulder. "Thanks, Bill."

He walked to where his horse was tied, lifted the saddle to its back, and tightened the girth strap. Then Alan swung up into the saddle and galloped toward the main fort.

Riding this narrow road always gave him a thrill. The view of the valley surrounded by high cliffs, from which dozens of watery veils plunged thousands of feet to the floor below, was a mesmerizing sight.

The domed peaks that towered above the rim were laden with snow so deep that the summer sun would be unable to melt it all away.

Ahead of him, the main fort's eastern gate opened as he approached. The guards waved him through. Alan noted that the walls were fully manned, an unusual occurrence with so much war preparation yet to be done, so rare that it only occurred during full battle rehearsals.

As he passed through the gates, another surprise confronted him. An entire company of the khan's riders sat on their horses in formation, lined up against the western wall facing into the courtyard, over a hundred riders strong. An odd trick of the late afternoon sunlight caught the reflections from the blades of their axes, which hung in straps from their saddles, sending multicolored glints spinning out into the eyes of onlookers.

Alan leapt from the saddle, tossed his reins to a groom, and strode rapidly toward the council chambers. As he entered the large room, he recognized the khan sitting beside his father, the two leaders deep in conversation. Also seated at the table were Gaar, Hanibal, and another of the khan's men, a striking warrior with long blond hair and beard whom Alan recognized. As Alan moved to the table, he thought he detected a sneer from Hanibal. That didn't surprise Alan. Their rivalry had its origin in Hanibal's belief that King Rodan should have given command of Tal's army to his father instead of Rafel. To Hanibal, the reason was as clear as it was unfair: Gaar held no noble title.

Movement pulled Alan's attention away from Hanibal. Rafel stood, an action repeated by all at the table.

"Alan. You know Khan and his son, Larok."

Alan stepped forward and extended his hand. "It is a pleasure."

Larok gripped his arm in a warrior's welcome. "Nay. The pleasure is mine."

Mandatory pleasantries out of the way, everyone seated themselves. Rafel looked at his son with a forced smile that left Alan cold. "Several weeks ago, Khan and I reached an agreement with great implications for both of our peoples. I believe it makes defeating the army of the protectors possible."

"Yes," said Khan. "Although the deep-spawned army from the lowlands is on its way to destroy you and your people, once they have finished with you, they will turn their attention to your neighbors. The protectors have long sought an excuse to take that which is mine. Having raised such an army, they will come for my people next. If we allow them to engage us one at a time, they will roll us up and we won't be able to stand against them. But together we have a chance to destroy this foul tide."

"As I said, we have agreed upon the terms and warranties involved in this alliance," Rafel continued.

"And this is where I come in?" Alan said.

"I am sorry that I didn't consult with you," said Rafel, "but yes. Khan has proposed that he leave his son and a platoon of his men with us. In exchange, I have agreed to send you and a platoon of our soldiers to accompany him back to Val'Dep."

Alan nodded, a numbness creeping up his spine. So he was being banished, prevented from being present to help defend the vale from the enemies that would soon crash against its defenses. From the slight smile on Hanibal's lips, the captain clearly liked this plan, a sentiment no doubt reflected among the vast majority of the soldiers, seeing as how they believed that fighting beside Alan was a direct ticket to the land of the dead. As he gazed into the captain's eyes, he had little doubt as to the source of that rumor.

Despite the bitter taste in his mouth, Alan responded with a clear and steady voice. "How long do I have to make ready?"

"Khan and his men will be my guests this evening. At dawn, you and a platoon of thirty soldiers will accompany Khan back to his fortress. Hanibal has already picked those who will go with you."

"I would ask that you add Bill Harrison to the list," Alan said, rising to his feet.

"Bill will go whether I like it or not," said Hanibal. "I might as well let him think it was my idea."

"Then if you will excuse me, I will prepare myself for travel."

Rafel hesitated but then slowly extended his hand. Alan gripped forearms with his father as he studied the high lord's face for any sign that he regretted the banishment that this act represented. Detecting no trace of emotion, Alan turned on his heel and strode from the room.

—⁓—

A dismal mood settled upon Rafel's shoulders like a lead-lined cape, causing them to slump. The sight of Alan riding away from Areana's Vale in the company of the khan hurt him even more than giving the order that had made it happen. As he had known would happen, Alan had not understood, and why should he? How would Rafel himself have felt if ordered to leave his people, to be unable to fight to defend them in a battle that might well be hopeless? Alan would think that his banishment was because a great number of Rafel's soldiers feared to have him fighting beside them on the walls.

The high lord kicked the heavy wooden bench that rested next to the massive table in his council chambers, sending it tumbling across the room. There could be no doubt that he had made the right decision, a decision that cemented the alliance between the vale and the people of Val'Dep, but that mattered little at the moment.

A commotion outside brought his head around as the door slammed inward, propelled with such force that it burst from its upper hinge. The heavy steel-strapped barrier sagged like a drunken innkeeper trying to close for the night. In walked Carol, eyes ablaze, her dark hair swirling in a breeze that moved with her. Arn strode purposefully in her wake, although he stopped to stand near the door, looking back out into the courtyard.

Captain Bannon, Rafel's personal guard, recovered in a flash and raced into the room, sword drawn. Arn moved as if in a blur, whirling under Bannon's sword, bringing Slaken up against the captain's throat and forcing him back against the wall.

"Captain Bannon," said Arn. "You know I've always liked you. Let's not do anything rash. Good to see you again, by the way."

"What in the deep?" Rafel yelled angrily, his gaze locking with Carol's.

"I do believe those were my exact words when I heard that you had ordered Alan away without bothering to inform me, not even to give me the chance to say goodbye."

Her words carried an outrage that Rafel had never heard from his daughter. He was stunned but immediately recovered his composure and turned to Bannon.

"Captain, leave us and ensure that I'm not disturbed."

Arn released the captain and resumed his place beside the entrance. Bannon nodded curtly and sheathed his sword, then left the room.

Rafel sat down heavily.

"For that, my daughter, I am deeply sorry. I negotiated the agreement with the khan weeks before you returned, and I could see no good way to break the news to Alan or to you. You've been uninvolved in any of the decisions of this vale for the last several months, even before you departed for the high mountains."

It seemed to Rafel that Carol's eyes went dead for a moment before softening. "Father, I am no longer the weak and broken girl that Arn carried out through your gates months ago."

"Yes, but it might have helped if, after your grand entrance, you had taken the time to tell me of your desire to participate in the leadership of our people once again."

"An invitation to your side might have hurried my steps in that direction."

Their gazes locked in mutually accusing stares.

"You want to know what I think?" interjected Arn.

"*No!*" The word came simultaneously from Rafel and Carol.

The self-conscious silence that followed was so comical that Carol reluctantly began to chuckle, a growing laugh that erupted in bursts between her reestablishment of a frown, sounding more like the croaking of a frog. The contagion spread to Rafel, who started harrumphing and snorting until tears rolled down his cheeks.

As they regained self-control, Carol threw her arms around her father's neck and whispered, "I missed you, Father."

Rafel swept her up in a bear hug, pressing his cheek to hers as his tears cut small streams that mingled with those from Carol's eyes. "I was afraid that I'd lost you."

Arn slipped out the door. For the longest time, Rafel held his daughter close, neither of them saying anything, immersed in the expression of feelings they had repressed for too long.

When at last Carol spoke, words flowed from her in a torrent that swept away the remainder of the morning and most of the afternoon. She described Misty Hollow. She spoke of how Arn had helped her master the magic described in the wielder's manuscript. Although she left out the details of what that magic involved, Rafel did not ask for more information.

For his part, Rafel recounted their preparations for war, the scouting reports, and how the people had come to regard Alan as the Chosen of the Dread Lord.

"That's terrible," she said.

"Yes, but you know how it is with rumors. You can't just put out an edict that no one's to believe them."

"I can," she said, her eyes flashing.

Distant thunder rumbled above the fort.

Rafel smiled and put his hand on her shoulder. "Somehow I don't think scaring them more will help. In time it will pass."

"If any of us has that much time."

"Speaking of that, and having seen for myself that you have fully recovered, I will issue the word today that I have restored you to my second-in-command, followed once again by Gaar."

"Fair enough." Carol rose and kissed his cheek. "It's time that I collect Arn and head home. We still have much work to do."

As she left the room, Rafel called after her. "Please tell that fiancé of yours to lay off almost killing my guards. It's a little hard on morale."

11

Areana's Vale
YOR 415, Early Spring

Arn paused to look around at what he and Carol had accomplished in just five days of hard work. They had managed to construct a shelter similar to what they used as a home in Misty Hollow. The space was located up an isolated canyon that branched out of Areana's Vale a league east of where Carol's cabin sat. They had required another two days to move all her things to their new home.

The decision to move to a different location was an easy one since it afforded much better security and privacy for Carol's mystical experimentation. The knowledge that the magic wielder was no longer directly in their midst also proved a great relief to the townspeople.

The couple's new home was nestled beneath an overhanging section of cliff, looking out over a magical vista, this one a narrow box canyon where a waterfall that plunged two thousand feet from the southern cliffs fed a rushing stream. And they had their own hot spring. Augmenting this luxury, the abundance of white aspen gave the canyon an otherworldly appearance.

When he had suggested that they model their home after the make-shift lodging they had created in Misty Hollow, Arn had not known how welcome the idea would be to Carol.

The separation from the common folk that populated the vale was ideal for her study and practice, and considering how short a time remained before the coming battles, she devoted herself to those activities.

A new worry crept into Arn's mind. Her powers had expanded so rapidly that he marveled at the things she could do with only an idle thought. Cook fires sprang to life as dinnertime approached. Small winds scuttled through their belongings, blowing away dust and leaving items neatly arranged as if of their own accord while Carol was engaged in deep meditation on other tasks.

Where control of such minor elementals before had involved concentration, they had now become her indentured servants, so fearful of angering the wielder that they strove to impress her with their devotion. It was as if she could see into their thoughts at a level that revealed their intent and that no amount of obfuscation could mask.

Elemental forces were not the only recipients of these new abilities. When Carol was moody, a quiet fell on their canyon, as if all living things had fled or cowered in their hiding places, fearing that the wrath of the gods themselves might smite them into the dirt. At such times, thunder rumbled above the canyon rim, and the wind moaned through the rock chimneys high above.

Carol experimented with these feelings, drawing forth her own emotions and using them to pull power from unknown recesses deep within her mind. What alleviated some of Arn's concerns was the way she brought herself back to the smiling woman he loved whenever he approached.

To say that her practice scared the deep out of anyone from the greater vale who happened to get curious and make their way into the

Fairy Rift, as his and Carol's canyon had come to be known, was an understatement.

Arn's threats to slowly cut pieces from their bodies until he grew tired of the sport did little to help the offenders with the task of recovering their equilibrium. For now, it suited his purpose that Carol and her surroundings be feared.

The thin trail of smoke from a cooking fire drifted lazily from their hearth, carrying with it the smell of roasting wild turkey. Carol ran to meet him, as excited as a schoolgirl. She threw her arms around his neck, kissing him with a vigor that transformed his hunger.

"Oh, Arn," she said, taking him by the hand. "I did it."

"What did you do, love?"

"I finally figured out the voices that have been mumbling in my head, the ones that made me think I was going crazy before, the ones I learned to block in Misty Hollow. I know what they are."

She paused, taking in a deep breath before continuing, the words bubbling out of her mouth in a rush.

"Arn, I can hear people's thoughts, feel their emotions, see their visions! I'm still not good at it, but most importantly I can block them out, thank heavens. There's so much that it would drive me crazy if I couldn't.

"It's like the babble in a large crowd, only worse. Images, sounds, feelings, tastes all flit across my senses from thousands of sources. I now see that the exercises from the ancient tome that deal with the pinpricks of light that surround me by the thousands are not only animals and elementals, but people, too. With people, it's much harder to filter them out, but I'm sure that with practice I'll be able to."

Arn stared at her, a great foreboding creeping into his heart. He reached out and took her gently by the shoulders, turning her to face him. "You haven't told anyone else about this, have you?"

"No," she said, her lips settling in a serious frown, "and I don't intend to."

"Listen to me. This new power of yours, you must keep it secret from everyone else. Not even your father or Alan can know of it. If anyone learns of it, the word will spread like a grass fire, and not only will everyone fear you, they will not tolerate you being near them."

"Believe me, I understand. I can imagine how people would feel if they think their deepest, darkest secrets are an open book to me. It wouldn't matter that this isn't how it works. They would believe I could look into their very souls.

"Instead, I think I only pick up the things they are consciously thinking, although even that's difficult, and I can't be sure that I'll ever get beyond that. I do seem to be able to influence the emotions of animals, and I would guess that I can also do so with people, at least somewhat. The possibilities are exciting, don't you think?"

"It scares the deep out of me."

Carol grabbed him by his shoulders and kissed him again. "You expect me to believe that, my love?"

"Well, it should scare me."

Suddenly Carol raised her head to look down toward the entrance to the canyon. "Kim's coming," she said. "I can't see her yet, but she is close."

Arn released Carol and stepped to the edge of the path that led up to their home. As if on cue, Kim stepped out of the woods and waved at them.

Arn and Carol made their way down the trail to meet her, which did not take long due to the speed at which the Endarian woman covered the ground in her graceful jog. The two women embraced, and then Kim thrilled Arn with a big hug as well.

"Oh," Carol said, "it's so good to see you. It feels like I was missing a piece of myself."

"I've missed you, too. Even the scruffy one."

Arn realized several days had passed since he had shaven.

"I was expecting you to call on me," Kim continued, "but when that didn't happen, I decided to check on your well-being." A reproachful frown settled upon her features.

Carol's face flushed. "I'm sorry. I've wanted to visit you ever since I got back. But with the need to get moved so that the people in Longsford Watch could sleep soundly, I dallied."

"You can blame me for that," said Arn.

"Oh, and I do," Kim said, although her mouth twitched with the hint of a smile. "No one could spend as much time as I spent with you, John, and Ty without noticing that you don't always prioritize social graces."

"Ouch," said Arn. "I know you came to catch up with Carol, so I'll excuse myself. I need to go discuss a few matters with High Lord Rafel."

As neither of the women objected, Arn turned and walked out of their canyon toward the lower fortress.

—᙮᙮—

By the time Arn made his way through the gates at the inner mouth of the gorge and traversed the various switchbacks of the line of defenses to arrive at the lower fortress wall, the sun had risen high enough to send its rays glimmering off the rushing stream that roiled down the deep canyon's bottom. His stride quickened as he approached his objective.

Something troubled him. The fortress was its normal hive of activity as soldiers and workmen bent their backs at their various tasks. On the walls above, an alert watch manned their positions. The sounds of sergeants and officers barking orders echoed between the rock walls.

High on the north wall of the canyon, two men toiled with a hammer and chisel along a narrow set of hand- and footholds carved into the cliff face. They worked to improve the access route to ledges that the soldiers had weakened. On Rafel's command, they could send these shelves crashing down onto forces jammed up before the fortress walls.

From where he stood, Arn could see one of the men gesturing to the other. The object of those gestures clung to the rock with both hands in a manner that Arn had seen many times before. He could practically feel the panic emanating from the man, frozen to the wall, several hundred feet above what was soon to become his grave.

Arn reached the canyon wall at a dead run, kicking off a small ledge two feet up, propelling his body upward to a handhold that he used to launch himself upward again. He landed atop a narrow ledge that provided a short pathway upward to an inch-wide crack that wormed its way up the cliff face. Alternately jamming fingers and the toe of a buckskin boot into the crack, he sprinted up the vertical climb.

He had lost sight of the men above, but the sounds that echoed down to him were not encouraging, the cascading rattle of small stones indicating that one or both must be slipping. Reaching the end of the convenient handholds provided by the crack, he was forced to slow his pace, each move on the rock now supported by only a couple of fingers or a toe. The thundering of his heart in his chest threatened to become loud enough to dislodge small boulders, but he redoubled his efforts to move faster.

As he once again crested a narrow ledge, the two soldiers came into view less than fifty feet above him. The bigger of the two had worked his way toward the frozen one and now extended himself outward with an outstretched hand, trying to grasp the other fellow's arm.

"No . . . Jonesy, you stay away from me. You're going to make me fall. Stay away!"

A sudden slippage of small stones accompanied the slimmer soldier's screams of panic and brought the efforts of the larger man to an awkward halt. Jonesy pitched forward so that his toehold failed, leaving him dangling from a single handgrip, feet scrabbling and searching for new purchase on the rock.

Arn directed his climb toward the smaller man, who continued to scream. The fellow had the better spot to hold on to but was rapidly losing his strength, having wasted so much effort clutching wildly in fear. As the gap closed, Jonesy slipped farther, and it became clear that he, too, was about to fall. Arn felt a wave of desire to save the braver of these two and let the panicked soldier fall. But perhaps he could save both. Arn reached out and grabbed the screamer, swinging his own body directly up against the young soldier's struggling form.

"Let me go! You're going to make me fall. Let go, I say!" he yelled, kicking out at Arn and losing his grip in the process.

The kick dislodged Arn's toehold so that he hung from a single hand, now supporting both his weight and the soldier's. Scissoring his legs, Arn gripped them around the soldier's body just beneath the armpits, releasing his one-handed grip on the fellow and regaining a double handhold on the rock, something that became more difficult to maintain as the lad struggled to clutch the rock wall.

"Be still!" Arn roared. "I have you."

Arn looked over at the bigger man, whose position continued to deteriorate as he struggled to regain his previous spot on the ledge above. "Hang on, Jonesy. I'll work my way over so you can use me as a foothold to push yourself up."

Arn pulled himself up, then switched grips with his right hand, regaining holds within reach of the large man. Jonesy grinned and swung his foot to use Arn's shoulder as a foothold, a move that never quite made it. As the man's boot neared Arn, the panicked lad he clung to with his legs reached out and grabbed it, attempting to pull himself up toward the ledge using Jonesy's body for support.

"Oh no." The words slipped from Jonesy's lips as his hands lost their grip on the ledge.

For a brief moment, Arn's arms exploded in agony as the weight of both men attempted to wrench him from the stone wall. Then Jonesy tumbled out and away, bouncing off the wall thirty feet farther down to spin onward, a limp puppet that repeatedly collided with stone outcroppings on his way down. The canyon echoed with the sound of damp thuds.

The soldier whom Arn clamped his legs around scrabbled on the rock, threatening to dislodge them both from the wall. That movement suddenly ceased when Arn released one handhold to slam the hilt of his knife into the side of the soldier's head. Returning the weapon to its sheath and regaining his grip, Arn wondered briefly if he had killed the lad, considered dropping him, and then reluctantly began climbing, hand over hand, down the cliff.

As he reached the ground, he loosed his grip on the soldier he had carried down the wall, freeing his legs once again and letting the youth's limp form crumple to the canyon floor. Arn settled on his feet, almost falling as the full weight of his exhaustion bent his knees and left his arms hanging like a pair of sausages.

He sagged backward against the rock wall he had just descended, working to bring his vision back from the narrow circle, surrounded by darkness, that seemed to want to snuff out the little center point of light. As his breathing slowed, Arn became aware of the hands that supported him at each shoulder, hands that belonged to Ty and John. They were saying something that he still could not quite make sense of.

"You crazy bastard," said Ty. "Why didn't you save the other guy instead of this little weasel who tried to kill you like he did the other fellow?"

Arn just shook his head, although the same thought had occurred to him numerous times on the way down.

As he looked around, he saw that a small group had gathered around the unconscious lad, men who were in a nasty mood. Several had begun taking turns shoving the unconscious soldier with a boot, trying to rouse the fellow.

"Newton! Wake up, you coward. You hear me?"

One of the men delivered a kick certain to leave a bruise.

Arn freed himself from Ty and John's grips and stepped forward into the circle of men gathered around the lad. "I'll cut the throat of the next man who does something like that. I didn't carry him down the cliff to have a mob kill him."

"Well, you should have dropped him," another fellow yelled. "He killed Jonesy as sure as we are all standing here, killed him from pure cowardice, the way we saw it."

Arn's eyes blazed. "Did I say anything about wanting a conversation? Listen, I'm going to say this only once: get back to your posts, or you'll join the dead fellow over there."

"What in the deep is going on here?"

The group parted at the arrival of Captain Hanibal, who quickly surveyed the scene and barked orders without waiting for a response to his question.

"Corporal Smith! I want these men put in formation and marched back to their posts immediately. Get two of them to carry Jonesy's body to the infirmary. Pick two others and have them take Newton there. I am going to have the ass of each one of this mangy crew who hasn't figured out what I mean by discipline and professionalism. Am I clear?"

"Yes, sir!" said a man whose face was as red as Hanibal's flaming mane.

"Then move!"

Hanibal strode to where Arn stood beside Newton. "I saw what you did up there. I've never seen the like."

He glanced down at Newton's unconscious body, now being lifted by two of the soldiers and carried away.

"Not being where you were, I'm not going to criticize the choice you made about who to save. I knew that kid was scared of heights, but I figured he would work through it. I sure didn't think he would panic."

"Some folks just can't get over it," said Arn. "I'm sorry about Jonesy, though."

Hanibal shook his head. "He was a very good man. Hate to lose that one."

With that he turned and followed the soldiers back toward the gates to the fort.

Arn watched him go, wondering what had driven him to make the choice he'd just made.

12

Galad looked out over the seemingly endless columns of Kragan's army as it sluggishly snaked northwest up the deep valleys toward the high country within which lay Endar Pass. With his fifteen hundred mist warriors well hidden among the trees of the forest, the time had come to slow the mass of vorgs and men even further. Their overwhelming numbers gave them confidence. Galad was about to impart a healthy dose of doubt.

"Laikas," he said to the time-shaper, "summon the mists."

She stared outward, her eyes taking on a faraway look as her hands and fingers traced intricate patterns in the air. Amidst the weaving, the fogs flowed. The passage of time slowed within the pomaly mists and accelerated in the rychly mists. And everywhere those mists flowed, what lay within disappeared.

Galad took one last look at the layout of Kragan's closest troops as the many variations of the mists obscured them, confirming that Laikas's channeling matched the pattern that Galad and his warrior brigade had rehearsed. He signaled to his subordinate commanders and led his warriors into the mists. As Galad stepped forward, he felt the slower zone he was leaving drag at his body. Within the variances of the rychly mists, Galad slowed his march to avoid getting far out in front of his warriors who had not yet entered the faster zone.

It was as if they stepped through translucent curtains. From Galad's perspective, he was never in a fog. When he stepped across a new boundary, it cleared, and the zone he had departed misted over. But all around him, other mists twisted and turned according to the will of the time-shaper who channeled them.

On his left, a light gray mist blocked his view back into the world where the normal passage of time held sway, while a few paces to his right, a faster rychly zone was a darker shade of gray. That variance in shade was one of the ways that mist warriors determined the best path to take. The lighter the mist, the slower time passed within. Galad cut across his current passage and transitioned into the next rychly zone, following a pattern that took advantage of the way Laikas's mists flowed.

The shape of these passages was critically important. It did a fighting group of mist warriors no good to move rapidly along a rychly passage that ran straight into a large enemy force. Thus, Laikas created a series of winding mists that hid the Endarians until the moment that they fell upon their enemy.

The time difference between adjacent mists could not be so large as to make the wall between them impenetrable. Galad and his fighters routinely operated in rychly mists, where time passed a half dozen times faster than normal, which was why mist warriors aged more quickly than other Endarians.

As Galad approached the area he had targeted for his main thrust, he pulled his bow off his shoulder and moved forward at a run. All around him, warriors followed their well-rehearsed paths, disappearing and reappearing as they wove their way through the subtle variations in the rychly fog.

—◊—

When the mists appeared, they flowed down from the high ridges to the northwest of Kragan's army. For days, he had been expecting just such an attack, but the Endarians had held back. The strategy had kept the vorgs and men who composed the bulk of his army on edge, costing them sleep. The scouting parties that Charna had sent out to find the Endarians had come back empty-handed or not come back at all.

Far behind his forward lines, Kragan called upon the air elemental Ohk, forming an invisible set of stairs that he climbed to a height of ten paces. From this perch, he studied what was happening to his leading troops. He had seen all this long ago when the Endarians had tried to destroy him and his treasured city of Lagoth. He licked his lips. This time he would teach them a lesson.

As the tendrils of mist penetrated into the front lines of his soldiers, Kragan saw the haze obscure hundreds of the Talian conscripts. A fireball arched into the sky, one of his wielders launching heat at the Endarian warriors likely to be moving within those mists. When it contacted the fogbank, the fireball deflected, exploding near its launch point, engulfing Kragan's nearby soldiers in flames. The sight pulled a curse from his mouth.

Kaleal's voice rumbled in his mind. *I see that one of your wielders did not pay attention when you instructed them that no elemental magic can penetrate the boundaries between time-mists.*

"Silap! I will deal with her later."

You may not get the opportunity.

Looking at the swath the fireball had cut through his troops, Kragan scowled. Normally he would not have placed a wielder near the front lines, but since elementals could only perform magic within the time zone within which they were summoned, Kragan needed to spread wielders throughout his columns. The Endarians suffered from similar limitations. They could only fight when they and their enemy shared the same rate of time's passage. That meant wielders needed to be with the troops whom the Endarians might attack.

A league to the north of where Kragan stood suspended in the air, the mists cleared, revealing a Talian company far ahead of where they should be. Kragan understood. They had been moving through what the Endarians called a rychly mist, where a time-shaper had accelerated time's passage. While they believed they marched forward at the same pace as their brothers-in-arms, they had advanced far beyond the rest of the army. But there was no sign of the Endarian warriors.

Then, as Kragan watched, another of the wispy tendrils consumed those forward troops. Finally. The start of the fight he had been anticipating.

As badly as he wanted to jump into the fray, now was the time to observe and learn how the commander of these mist warriors operated. For that knowledge, Kragan would gladly sacrifice as many Talian conscripts as necessary.

—⁓—

A hundred of his troops formed a single rank with Galad at its center as he studied the nuances of the mist. The vision that formed in his mind confirmed that this was the place to launch his attack. As he raised his bow in preparation for stepping into the time-mist that Kragan's soldiers now occupied, his warriors mirrored his motion.

They strode forward as one, feeling the pressure that went with stepping from a faster zone into a slower one. To the eyes of their enemies, his warriors would appear to have stepped through a curtain at normal speed. But the vorgs and men who made up that foul army could not anticipate when or from which direction the attack would come.

As the pressure normalized, the mists rolled away to reveal a close approximation of what Galad had expected. The march of several hundred of Kragan's troops had faltered as they looked about in confusion.

In rapid succession, Galad's warriors launched three volleys of arrows, concentrated upon the area occupied by one of Kragan's magic wielders and the soldiers who protected him. Then without waiting for the enemy response, Galad turned and stepped back into the rychly mist from which he had just come, accompanied by his hundred warriors. The mist he left behind clung to him, striving to prevent him from entering a space where he could move more freely. As soon as he freed himself from the fog that tugged at his backside, Galad raced to his right, getting clear of the area where the enemy archers were sure to return fire, knowing that he and his warriors moved fast enough to get away before any arrows could emerge from the slower zone.

Glancing back, he saw a storm of arrows slowly emerge into the zone where time passed at a much quicker pace. But the transition had robbed them of most of their momentum. Too late and off target, they dropped to the ground at a fraction of the distance they would have traveled had they not made the transition. Other arrows slowly sprouted from the mist as Kragan's archers began firing wildly in all directions, but Galad and his warriors easily avoided their paths. As the storm of shafts died out, Galad signaled for his warriors to ready for the attack. Once again they raised their bows, but this time they did not move back into the slowing fog. Instead, they waited.

A sudden rush of human warriors clawed their way into the rychly zone, but as they fought themselves clear of the thick soup that bound them, Endarian arrows suddenly pierced their necks and other areas where their armor was insufficient to deflect the flying barbs. Mist-warriors, who had exchanged their bows for Endarian swords, rapidly dispatched those humans who fought their way out of the clinging soup.

Once more Galad signaled his troops, and they followed him into yet another of the rychly mists as a pomaly zone flowed in behind them, further isolating the confused human survivors. Racing along the winding path that led back to the mountain forest from which he had launched the attack, Galad felt satisfied with all that his company had just accomplished.

Emerging into normal time, concealed by the thick woods, he and his warriors were the first to arrive at the rally point he had designated. Over the next hour and a half, the other companies emerged from the mists to join him. By the time all his commanders had reported in, the tally had become clear. Except for one company that had emerged from the mists into a storm of fireballs and lightning from two of Kragan's wielders, casualties had been light. But the losses among that unfortunate company had been horrific. Only twenty-three of those warriors had survived. Almost all of that contingent who had struggled back to the rally point were wounded. And their company commander, Jalen, was among the fallen.

Shunting aside the sorrow that he would allow himself to feel once his brigade was safely away, Galad led his remaining warriors, still more than thirteen hundred strong, out of the foothills and back into the Glacier Mountains. Although today he had inflicted far more casualties on Kragan's army than he had sustained, he knew it was only the bite of an annoying fly. Next time, he would have to do better.

13

Arn found himself seated atop Ax, gazing down the ridgeline to the west, the same general direction that he scanned for any sign of motion. Arn could feel Slaken occupying its customary place, strapped in a sheath at his side. Today it tugged at him, the four elementals bound within the runes on its haft hungering for the lives that the weapon would take in the coming days.

He drew the big knife from its sheath, turning it over in his hands to study it.

Slaken was his one magical possession, its very existence as ironic as his own. The dull blade, darker than a starless night, absorbed light rays, leaching them into the handle. There they warped and twisted, dancing along the strange runes carved into its surface. The effect was fluid, as if light flowed along the narrow channels the script cut into the weapon's landscape.

Overcome with gratitude that Arn had saved the life of his only son, King Rodan of Tal had granted him the right to have any one thing the monarch could give. What Arn had asked for had taken Gregor,

Rodan's magic wielder and the kingdom's chief armorer, years to make: the black blade with the carved handle, a handle with so many magical runes that one blended into the next.

The blade was so magical that it had no magic, offering sorcery so twisted in upon itself that one spell blocked another until none worked. In fact, no spell had any effect upon the knife, nor upon the person who had made the blood-bond with the weapon, and only Arn could hold the blade. Slaken gave Arn the one thing he desired most in the world— the ability to operate without the direct interference of wielders.

Arn pulled himself from the trance where his study of the runed haft had placed him, turning his thoughts back to the task that Rafel had assigned him in a sudden meeting.

Arn's departure from Areana's Vale had happened so suddenly that it had left a hollow ache in his heart, along with a growing dread. Carol had been present at the meeting with Rafel and Gaar, and even though no one had disagreed with the course of action that the high lord had decided upon, the decision was painful for both Arn and Carol. The thought of being sent on a mission that separated him from the loved one he had vowed to protect made him physically ill.

The rangers had spotted the lead scouts of the army of the protectors no more than two days west of Areana's Vale. As he sat atop his mount, Arn knew that the horde would be reaching the outer boundaries of the Great Forest in a few hours. Moving fast and recklessly, they were seeking early contact with Rafel's scouts.

Such was not to be. The high lord had given the order that he wanted no advance contact with the enemy lead elements. He wanted to let them enter the narrow ravine at full speed so that when they hit the walls of the lower fortress, they would be well beyond the assistance of the main body of their army.

Before that happened, though, he wanted Arn out of the vale.

The plan made sense. Carol would position herself high on an outcropping behind the fortifications, where everyone could see her clearly.

There she would make her magical stand, giving hope to friendly forces and striking fear into the heart of the enemy.

The downside was that she would face constant mystical assault from every spell-casting priest the protectors could throw at her. They would attempt to kill her first and, failing that, keep her so busy that she could not help with the main battle.

That led to Arn's mission. As much as he wanted to be near Carol and protect her during the fight, it made more sense for him to be away from the canyon before the enemy forces blocked the exit. In that way, he could infiltrate behind their lines, killing as many of the priests as possible before and during the fight—the best way to help even the odds, which were so heavily stacked against his true love.

He spurred the horse forward into a ground-covering canter, directly toward the line of giant trees that spread out north and south just a league in front of him. The powerful beast moving beneath him, the creak of the leather saddle, and the musty smell of horse sweat all brought back feelings that he had not felt for a long time, heightening his awareness.

He entered the first of the long shadows that blocked the orange rays of the sinking sun. Entering the wood line, he turned south, the sound of his passing muffled in the deep needles that the mighty evergreens had deposited over the millennia. He wanted to make haste in order to bypass the protectors' army to the south.

All through the night he rode, though darkness slowed his progress to a steady trot. An hour before dawn, he passed out of the Great Forest, entering a set of rolling hills and broad valleys. The birds ignored his passage, or perhaps their boisterous conversations were about him. Whatever the true nature of their calls, the volume of their singing was impressive, as though they were determined to make everyone aware that spring had arrived and it was time to celebrate.

Looking out to the west, a great valley spread out away from him, with herds of deer grazing casually along with antelope and the strange wooly cattle that frequented these lower altitudes. None of the animals showed any of the concern that they would exhibit if masses of vorgs or armies of soldiers moved anywhere near them. Arn turned west.

Once again he quickened the pace, racing into the west on the back of Ax, who had never tired in all the times that Arn had sat astride him. Muscle rippled beneath skin like bunches of wire, a visual effect that did nothing to enhance the handsomeness of the horse but which whispered of unimaginable reserves of power and endurance.

The sun passed overhead in its great arc, not directly, but a bit to the south, reaching its zenith as Arn turned back to the north. He paused at a small stream to water the horse and to refill his water pouch, and then he was racing northward once more. He moved back into the rolling hill country, hills covered with juniper on the north side but which were mostly barren of trees on the sunny southern side. Rounding the military crest of one of these, he spotted the vorgs.

A group of twenty warriors raced southward, running in formation with great urgency. Arn dismounted, tying Ax in the trees and slipping forward to a spot where he could watch them unseen. This enemy patrol made no sense. Why was an elite hunter-killer platoon on some urgent mission racing in the wrong direction? From the look of them, they were an exceptional unit, all big, heavily armored, and well disciplined—a very unusual setup for vorgs. They were after someone or something.

Arn wondered if he had been spotted. It was possible, but doubtful. These vorgs looked like they knew exactly where they were heading, and it wasn't toward him. Most likely they had some talisman that served as a compass guiding them to their quarry, the sort of thing the priests could have provided them.

He knew he should get moving, but something bothered him, worry worming into his mind in a way that he could not ignore. Something bad was about to happen. A sudden headache hammered his temples so that his vision blurred, producing a cold sweat that poured from his brow.

He had to get moving north again. Carol needed him. He could not let her fight alone the dozens of priests that would engage her. But as he looked back at the running formation of vorgs, his intuition would not let him resume his original task. For some reason, that small vorg battle group posed a greater threat to the love of his life than all the protectors combined.

Though the decision was chewing his guts out, he would leave Carol to fend for herself. A thought filled him with fury and frustration. Was Slaken playing with his intuition, making him act rashly? After all, Carol had said that the four elementals bound within its runes were full of rage. Did they want her dead just to punish him?

He wavered, analyzing his feelings. No. The call that pushed him to pursue the vorgs came from within himself. The tug of his intuition had never betrayed him.

With a kick of his heels, Arn turned to follow the vorgs south.

14

The *swoosh-thunk* of an arrow embedding itself in wood pulled Rafel's attention. A lone arrow, the shaft shattered from impact, was embedded in the log wall of the fort. High on the north rim of the canyon, a man with a bow waved and disappeared from view. Derek Scot had come up with the idea for the ingenious battlefield messaging system and had been assigned to lead the ranger platoon whose task was to make it work.

A group of fifteen rangers had made the four-day ride out of the vale and up through the high passes to the tops of the cliffs. These men were now spread out in high observation posts along the western tops of those cliff walls, five thousand feet above where Rafel stood, so that they could observe what was happening in the lowlands leading up to the canyon entrance.

As needed, Derek would dispatch a messenger to a point where he could fire an arrow down into selected locations in the lower fortifications, where the attached note would be retrieved and relayed to Rafel, Gaar, or Hanibal.

Duncan, Rafel's aide, climbed down the ladder, retrieved the note attached to the broken shaft of the arrow, and returned to Rafel's side at the top of the outermost defensive wall of the lower fort. Rafel perused the message and turned to Gaar and Hanibal, who stood near him atop the fortifications.

"A disorganized group of several hundred vorgs and men have reached the entrance to the canyon, running hard with no thought of waiting for the main forces far behind them. They'll be on us in about a half hour. Signal the high archers that I don't want them engaged until they hit the wall right here.

"Hanibal, you have the forward command. Remember, let them hit this wall. When you open fire, that will be the signal for the archers you have positioned along the higher trails to open up with their enfilading attack. I don't want any of the rockslides used. You will only release those once several thousand vorgs are jammed up in the canyon below the forts."

"Understood," said Hanibal, turning to relay orders to his subordinate commanders.

Rafel turned back toward Gaar, noting the swift gaze of pride that crinkled the weathered stone of the old warrior's face in an almost imperceptible shift. If he had not known his comrade so well, he might have believed that he imagined the sight.

"The people of the Kanjou tribe?" he asked.

"The last of our cliff-dwelling neighbors passed through our upper gates and were taken to their camp in the vale more than an hour ago," said Gaar. "It was mainly the elderly in the last group. I gather that Chief Dan had considerable difficulty in convincing several of the ancient ones to leave their cliff homes. The last report said that a couple of dozen stayed behind despite his efforts."

"That is sad but not surprising. Some folks would rather die than flee, and others just won't believe what's about to happen." Rafel sighed. "They're as good as dead now."

He looked around. It was a good strong fort. They had not built their defenses from stone, but log walls were strong, and they would have to do. The clatter of metal filled the air as soldiers moved about in their chain mail, bearing ironbound shields, fine steel swords, and the occasional bit of plate armor.

Troops clustered together atop the battlements, shoulder to shoulder. Bowmen filled all the slotted firing positions, with more archers positioned in higher places farther to the rear.

Along the tight paths they had cut into the face of the cliff, bowmen manned firing positions that were beyond the outer fortress walls. These positions were difficult to get to and difficult to assault, and they provided no means to retreat from battle. The men who fought there knew that they would have little chance of surviving the main assault.

Even farther out and higher on the cliffs, above places where the enemy would jam up during the main fight, boulders had been undercut so that they could be dislodged by a single man, generating rockslides to plunge into the gorge below. Soldiers manned all of these high positions, but Rafel had no intention of using them in the initial fight.

The midmorning sun beat down hot today, although Rafel recognized that most of his heat came from the chain and plate armor he wore over his leather clothing. War was never a comfortable thing and grew more uncomfortable as he aged. Or perhaps his memory inflated the glory of battles past and minimized the aches and pains he had endured.

He and Gaar separated, making the rounds of the men, patting them on the back, shaking their hands, giving the words of encouragement that leaders were meant to give to those who would soon struggle for their lives and the lives of their loved ones. Rafel knew that their hearts now thrummed in their chests as adrenaline surged through their veins, leaving a sick feeling of anticipation and dread. Together they endured that most difficult of all parts of battle, the waiting before combat began.

Rafel looked back up the canyon toward Areana's Vale, toward the jutting ledge that extended outward from the southern wall just to the east of the uppermost of the layered sections of the canyon defenses, to the spot where Carol would make her stand. He had ordered her to remain away for the first skirmish. She needed to rest for the subsequent battles.

The lonely ledge where his daughter would present herself as destroyer and target filled his soul with terror. How many of the priests had Arn said the protectors could muster against her? Over a hundred? Perhaps many more, some powerful in their own magics while others were mere novices.

His only consolation was the thought of Arn finding his way to the heart of the most dangerous of these enemies. He had sent forth his most deadly weapon, the assassin who had never failed him in all the years of their acquaintance and one who was devoted to Carol's safety. No, Arn would not fail them.

The warbling sound of a horn was accompanied by a rattling chorus of armor as every man in the fortress straightened at the sound. Vorg war horns were hardly things of beauty either to behold or hear, carved as they were from human femurs and sounding something akin to the squeal of a wild hog.

Rafel climbed to the command deck, a raised platform behind the main wall but elevated so that he could survey the entire scene through a slotted turret that jutted forward, providing views along a variety of angles. Much as he wanted to be on the main wall for this first attack, it made no sense for either himself or Gaar to do so. A time would come when his sudden arrival at the forward wall would bolster men whose hopes had faded, but this was not that time. This was Hanibal's time.

The lead vorgs had rounded the bend in the canyon about half a league to the west of the fort. This first group slowed as they were forced to cross the stream, swollen by spring runoff. It plunged through the gorge in a fury of rapids, switching back and forth across the canyon's width. By the time the entire group managed to cross, their numbers had swollen to several hundred as stragglers from behind caught up.

The sound of the horns grew as more vorgs arrived and made the crossing, stretching out along the narrow slivers of land that led beside the stream toward the fort that rose up to block the canyon to the east.

Rafel watched as Hanibal and his commanders worked the line of defenders on the wall, passing among the men, reinforcing their orders with repetition.

"Hold. Do not fire until I give the command."

Gaar moved up beside Rafel. "Something isn't right here."

"I see it," Rafel said. The vorgs had stopped their headlong advance a little over a quarter league from the fort. "I've never known vorgs to be able to hold like that when their blood was up."

"There," Gaar said, pointing to a spot behind where the vorgs were gathering. A lone rider in a dark cloak trailed behind them, stopping at a point where he could gaze up the canyon toward the fort.

"Ah. Not quite as stupid as we thought. Our enemy sent a priest to ride herd on this lot. He's wanting to draw us out, to force us to come out and engage this bunch forward of the fort."

"Or he's waiting for reinforcements," said Gaar.

Rafel turned to Duncan. "Get Carol up here."

The young aide leapt down the ladder, disappearing along the winding street below.

By the time Carol climbed onto the command deck, the number of vorgs had grown to almost one thousand. They had moved into formation, picking up a guttural chant with the banging of shields serving as percussion accompaniment. The priest sat his mount a hundred paces behind their formation.

"I think they want to draw me out," Carol said. "They're using these vorgs as bait so they can see how I confront them magically."

"If we do nothing," said Rafel, "they'll study our defenses while they wait for the arrival of the main force."

Carol closed her eyes, moving into the trancelike state that the high lord had seen before. The charge began with just two vorgs, but it was like the crack in the dam that, once breached, brought forth a flood. The vorgs howled and charged, actions that were transmitted to those adjacent to them so rapidly that it seemed as if all the invaders made up their minds as one. The priest in the back gestured wildly, but they paid no heed.

"What happened?" asked Rafel.

"Something they didn't expect," said Carol, opening her eyes.

"Hold!" Hanibal's command rang out like the toll of a steeple bell. When the first of the vorgs reached the wall, swinging grappling hooks on ropes, he gave another command. "Fire!"

The archers unleashed a volley from atop the walls, and a wave of vorgs fell. Another volley of arrows from the cliffs behind the invaders raked their flanks. Several grappling hooks lodged on the top of the main wall, but soldiers severed the lines with sword and ax. The vorgs spread out along the wall on a thirty-pace stretch of land that separated the cliff from the raging mountain stream.

Several tried to work their way around the log wall and across to the far bank, but a swarm of arrows from the section of fort that obstructed the stream's south bank bit into them. Others fell into the rapids, where the fury of the torrent pulled them under the roiling waters.

The vorgs who made it to the base of the fortress next to the stream engaged in a brief but furious exchange of arrows with Hanibal's archers, but fell without making their way to the top of the walls.

Movement in the distance drew Rafel's gaze as the priest turned his horse and fled, his dark cloak flapping behind him as he rode. A single bolt of lightning split the sky, sending horse and rider tumbling into the stream, not to reemerge.

The remaining vorgs ran. As they broke away from the walls, Hanibal raised his sword, and the winch crew lowered the drawbridge, spewing forth a hundred of Rafel's cavalry. They charged out after the fleeing warriors, their bodies flung low across the necks of their warhorses. In minutes, the battle was over, an eerie stillness replacing the cacophony that had preceded it.

"Duncan, get me a report on our wounded and killed. Also, tell Hanibal I want the vorgs stripped of any useful weapons, especially crossbows, bows, and arrows. Then I want their heads placed atop spears and stuck in the ground between here and the mouth of the canyon. Tell him to post outriders and be quick about it. I don't want them caught out in the open."

As Duncan departed, Rafel turned to Carol. "Do you mind telling me what you did there?"

"Let's just say I ruffled their feathers a bit. Now if you don't need me, I'll return to my preparations for the battle that is yet to come."

Rafel stared at his daughter for a moment, but as it became obvious that no further information on this subject would be forthcoming, he waved her away. He was familiar with wielders calling forth lightning, wind, and fire. However, the way Carol had caused the vorgs to defy the priest and attack made the hair on the nape of his neck stand straight out.

As he watched Carol climb down the ladder, he realized that he did not want to know what power she had just wielded.

—⚌—

Carol watched as nightfall draped the battlements, an inkiness penetrated only by the twinkling pinpricks of the stars in the rift of sky. The strict light discipline exercised by Rafel's forces gave mute testimony to his soldiers' training. No one lit a torch nor struck flint to steel. Within the lower fort, night reigned supreme.

Deafening noise echoed from the ravine's walls. The army of the protectors had entered the lower section of the canyon in late afternoon, and although they had not yet made their way around the nearest switchbacks, the hammering of their drums and chants now rose in volume so that the canyon vibrated in accompaniment.

The first ripples of torchlight skittered across the rocks at the near bend in the canyon, dim creepers followed by the glow of hundreds of torches. The light crawled across thousands of figures that jammed both sides of the roaring stream. Dread radiated outward from the scene, sending chills up Carol's spine.

The horde lay great ramps across the stream and poured over them. Still a half league west of the lower fort, they moved inexorably forward, dragging with them siege engines, ladders, and more wooden ramps.

Gasps and murmurs whispered along the tops of the fortress walls. They subsided as the leaders moved among their men, bolstering their will with the confidence of old soldiers who masked their fear at the scene unfolding beyond their walls.

With a thought, Carol bathed the top of the stone pinnacle in a soft radiance. She stood gallantly, her long-sleeved white blouse hanging loosely over her leather riding pants, her white cape swirling in a gentle breeze, arms upraised for all to see. Beside her, clad in her color-shifting uniform that had changed to brown, sat a peaceful Kim, her long auburn hair framing her features. A cheer arose from the battlements, and Carol amplified the sound so that it crashed back and forth between the cliffs, loosing rivulets of stone, which rattled down to the canyon floor.

In answer to her casting, clouds boiled over the cliffs above the vorgs, webbed by sheet lightning. The building storm surged toward her.

The leading edge of the horde reached a point just a hundred paces beyond the walls of the lower fort and halted in a mass that suddenly bristled with bows. The torchbearers moved among them, and a thousand arrows blazed with fire.

Carol gestured, and the flames died. Then the storm erupted. Lightning bolts cascaded onto her pinnacle, accompanied by thunder that shook the stone beneath her feet.

The bolts struck at Carol like angry snakes but failed to penetrate the translucent orb that shielded the two women. Electrical energy crawled along the glittering surface of the bubble, ever seeking but finding no inward path.

A horn blared from within the lower fort, and Rafel's archers launched volley after volley from the tops of its ramparts, cutting a swath through the vorgs below as lightning illuminated the battlefield. The enemy archers released their arrows, but without the burning brands, they had little effect upon the defenders.

The protectors focused their sorcery on trying to dislodge Carol from her lofty perch, but she struck back, sending a fireball into the stream beside them. The resulting jet of superheated steam threatened to envelop them, but they deflected it directly into a group of their soldiers, cooking the vorgs inside the shells of their armor. The smell of roasted meat wafted through the rift, carried aloft on the wind.

Carol longed to lash out with all her might to decimate the foul beings crammed into the visible part of the gorge, but she could not allow the priests to sap her strength, not while they kept the vast bulk of their army in reserve. The small group of protectors, against whom she now sparred, were but a probe that their high priest had sent to test and tire her.

The vorgs reached the closed drawbridge, the weight of the mob pressing forward until the wood cracked under the pressure. Rafel's archers targeted the ladder bearers, their fires so effective at killing the incoming horde that only the crews protected by wooden ramps reached the outer walls. As groups of humans and vorgs raised the ramps into position, Hanibal's troops poured forth buckets of grease.

Swordsmen with good footing met the first of the slipping and sliding vorgs to reach the top of the wall. As those vorgs fell, their blood added to the slipperiness of the ramps. These soon became so slick that the invaders only managed to make their way forward across the backs of their fellows. The cluster of ramps against the walls left few places for more ladders, jamming up the assault so that a great mass built in the canyon below.

Suddenly something surged through that mass. Three of the thickly muscled, ten-foot-tall humanoids known as gruns trampled the vorgs before them, crushing their way toward the raised drawbridge. Ignoring the volleys of arrows that buzzed into their hides, the gruns reached the closed portal, battering it with their powerful arms and shoulders. The thick wood cracked and splintered.

Carol launched a series of fireballs at the protectors, forcing them to throw up a shield of their own. Then she shifted her attack, hurling lightning bolts into the gruns, sending their charred bodies crashing to the ground. However, the damage they had inflicted on the drawbridge had severely weakened it.

Again the priests struck out at her, forcing her to strengthen her own shielding. As she did, a group of running vorgs raced forward, carrying a metal-tipped log, shattering the weakened planks and opening a six-foot-wide hole into the lower fort. Carol watched in horror as the vorgs flooded into the gap.

—⚏—

Angloc wore the cloak of Jaradin Scot's body with long familiarity, moving through the darkness with the stealth of a ghost. The spell was a simple one. He had merely to summon the air elemental Nematomas to cloak his body with invisibility. The protector was easily able to slip away from the crowd of soldiers during the fighting. In the midst of all the ensuing commotion of the battle, he had crept eastward through the upper two forts that blocked the ravine that led into Areana's Vale, crossing each drawbridge in turn.

Inside his core, he fumed, his guts writhing. The witch on the pinnacle had robbed him of what was rightfully his. How many days and nights had he snuck away to creep in close to Kim, watching her bathe?

He had even snuck into her cabin to watch her make love to her little weasel of a lover, which had almost driven him to kill John and take her right there atop his bloody corpse.

It wasn't duty that stopped him, even though his duty weighed heavily upon him. Fear was what stayed his hand, although it was not fear of the witch of the vale. Nothing in this miserable hole inspired fear in him.

But fear of the master, that was another thing entirely. None who had intimately beheld Krylzygool could do aught but tremble at the dark god's wrath. Therefore Angloc had held himself in check so that he could play his part in the upcoming battle, all the while consoling himself with the knowledge that he would make this Endarian woman his plaything when the time was right, when it would not spoil everything.

Tonight was to be the night, that perfect time when, in the midst of the battle confusion, he could entice Kim away with a summoning.

But the witch had ruined everything. Who would have thought that she would keep Kim beside her in the battle? The selfish bitch had confiscated the Endarian to draw upon her healing powers, not letting her bastard half sister tend to the soldiers who were even now fighting and dying far below the spire upon which the two women perched. The strategy was something he himself would have employed. He had been an imbecile to fall for the myth that Carol was somehow different and would give herself selflessly for her people. What an absolute fool he had been.

Angloc passed through the last of the canyon forts like a midnight caress, a whisper that raised the hair on the necks of a few guards, causing them to glance around nervously. Moving out through the eastern-most gate, the priest turned south, going around the base of the section of cliff that branched away from the main wall to form the spire upon which both the object of his desire and the target of his malice maintained their lofty purchase. Finding the steep trail that led up the back side, he started to climb.

Okay. He would simply have to reorder his plans. Kill the witch first, then take the Endarian. A ragged smile distorted his features. This could work out far better than he had imagined. How would it go? Jaradin Scot arrives at the top of the spire with a critical message from High Lord Rafel. Carol lets him inside her defenses, and as he steps close to whisper the message, he shoves his dagger deep into her throat.

Then, high above the battle, where all could see, he would bathe them in a different kind of light than that of the white witch. The bloodred glow would let all watch him toss down one of Rafel's daughters and then take his sweet time with the other. All the while, Krylzygool's army would parry with the disheartened defenders below.

His heart thrummed in his chest as he picked up the pace. Yes. This was going to be sweet.

15

"What?" Alan bellowed, causing the khan's guards to reach for their weapons.

"You will do as I command," said Khan, holding out his arms so that his squire could finish fastening his chest plate in place. "Your father sent you here in exchange for my son, that each of us could have a piece of ourselves in the other's home. As we speak, all but a few of my able-bodied warriors sit mounted on the plain below, ready to ride with me to the aid of your people, but you will not be among them. You will continue, as my son continues, to reside in the house of the other, spilling your blood only in defense of the other and not in defense of your own."

Alan felt the veins in his neck bulge, as if the blood inside them boiled.

"Much as you want to fight for your people, you will stay here and defend mine on the off chance that I should fail and the vorg attack turns toward this stronghold. One of my blood fights for your people.

One of Rafel's blood shall stand ready to do the same for mine. So the two of us have spoken. So shall it be."

"If you fail, then we'll all die anyway," said Alan. "Counting my thirty soldiers, you can only leave a couple of hundred warriors behind to protect several thousand women, children, and old men. Even these mighty battlements cannot stand against such a force as the protectors will throw against them."

"What you say may be true, but I will not leave them undefended by a man of royal blood. There are two of us here of royal blood—you, the son of the leader of your people, and myself. If I am not to stay, then you must."

The khan grasped his helm and battle-ax and turned back to Alan. "Make the most of the time that you have. Get my people ready for whatever may come. I must leave them in your hands as you must leave your people's fate in mine. Let us not disappoint each other."

Alan felt rooted to the floor as he watched the khan stride from the room, picking up a cadre of warriors as he departed, his squire trailing behind.

Having forgotten Ty's presence, Alan suddenly noticed that the barbarian had moved up beside him.

"We all have our tasks," Ty said. "Don't make the mistake of underestimating those that your father and the khan have assigned you."

Then Ty turned and strode from the room, following in the khan's wake.

Shrugging free of his imagined fetters, Alan moved to the balcony of the khan's council chamber. It perched high on the wall of a tower that afforded a masterful view of the valley beyond the outer walls of the fortress. Spread out upon that plain, several thousand horsemen stoically sat atop their mounts, long hair and beards hanging down over shoulder and chest, battle-axes slung across their backs or hanging in straps from their saddles.

"*Khan!*"

The cry echoed off the stone walls of the fortress as the khan appeared atop his warhorse, riding out on the causeway below. With no pause, he lengthened the steed's stride to a gentle canter, sweeping along the front ranks of his men and then looping back, toward Areana's Vale. From right to left the companies of riders fell in behind him, forming a mighty column of death on horseback, a column that soon disappeared around the bend to the south, leaving a yawning maw of silence in its wake. Alongside them rode the shirtless Kanjari.

Alan felt he should have been among them. It was all he could do to keep from riding out after Ty. But such an act would only let his father down once again.

16

Glacier Mountains, Southeast of Endar
YOR 415, Mid-Spring

As Ohk created a magical lens that served as his far-glass, Kragan watched the forward edge of the battle unfold before his eyes. For these weeks that the Endarian mist warriors had nipped at his flanks, Kragan's forces had failed to crush them. Their time-shaper had proven to be a true master of the craft, slicing off chunks of Kragan's army, confusing and isolating groups of soldiers so that the Endarians could sweep in and destroy them. Kragan had even lost two of his wielders to the attacks. But the men and vorgs whom Kragan had sacrificed had served their intended purpose. These battles had revealed a subtle pattern in the master time-shaper's magic.

Kaleal's thoughts whispered in his head. *Dalg awaits your command.*

"First we wait and observe. Only after confirmation will I strike."

As the time-mists rolled down from the forested hillside to the northwest of the lead elements of Kragan's army, Charna signaled for those troops to charge. It was a mad move that would only play into the hands of the mist warriors' commander. In the next few hours, thousands of Talian conscripts would die within the fogs. But as Kragan hoped, the Endarian time-shaper reacted with an eagerness to enfold those who charged within her nebulous tentacles. And the pattern of those tendrils allowed Kragan to determine from whence they flowed.

Kragan called forth Ohk to encase his head in an air bubble that would keep him alive for the duration of what he now needed to do. He then ensnared Dalg, feeling the ground below acquire the consistency of air, dropping his primordial body ten paces beneath the surface before the stone solidified beneath his feet. As he strode forward, he forced Dalg to make the earth through which he passed acquire a brownish, gray-tinged transparency, allowing Kragan to see.

Feeling his throat tighten in anticipation, the sorcerer threw himself forward at a run, creating a furrow in the ground that solidified behind him and sending out a tremor that startled the soldiers who felt it. Within Kragan's head, Kaleal's snarl rumbled.

—⟪⟫—

Standing in the midst of the swirling fog that flowed from her out-stretched palms and fingers, Laikas felt the ground tremble. Clad in the same color-shifting Endarian uniform worn by Galad and the other warriors, she paused in her weaving of the mists. Her eyes roamed left and back to the right, seeing only the sunlit hillside glade within which she stood. The urge to glance back over her shoulder caused her to spin in place. But again, there was nothing to cause her concern.

Here in this glade, time passed at twice the normal rate, much slower than the mists within which Galad's warriors moved. But this temporal zone formed a balanced progression, optimizing her ability to channel both the rychly and slower pomaly vapors. It also provided her excellent boundaries from which she could sense the disturbances within the shrouds she had created.

As she turned her attention back to the evolving pattern that Galad was counting on her to continue to weave, a loud rumble caused her to spin around just in time to see a head and a pair of clawed hands sprout from the ground. For a mere handful of seconds, the sight of those slitted golden eyes in a face of unnatural beauty froze her in place as the being struggled to emerge. Its lips parted to reveal the incisors of a great cat, the expression startling Laikas back to her senses.

In desperation, she shifted her channeling, only to cry out in agony and despair as icy limbs formed in the air around her, locking her body in place. Unable to make the motions required to summon new mists that would allow her to escape, she was forced to watch the being, who stood a head taller than she, step forward. Caressing her frozen cheek with a bronze hand, the primordial leaned in until she could feel his hot breath. She breathed in his musky scent and felt her heart stutter in her chest.

Laikas managed a husky whisper. "Who are you?"

"Some call me Kragan. Others name me Kaleal. It matters not, for now we are one."

The horror that filled her soul at this admission lent Laikas one last burst of strength. But as she flexed her fingers to open a mist channel, the claws on that bronze hand ripped out her throat.

—w—

Galad swept in and out of fog, his elegantly inscribed sword spraying blood in an arc as he and his warriors wreaked havoc on the thousands of confused enemy soldiers who struggled to get clear of the clinging pomaly mist. As if in a carefully choreographed dance, he moved forward and back, whirling into strikes that severed limbs and heads, his long tresses whipping about him. Those of his enemies who managed to get all the way into the rychly mist, within which Galad fought, found themselves underprepared and overmatched.

Raw terror filled the eyes of many of the human soldiers who tried to reenter the fogbank from which they had just emerged, only to be shoved back by those still trying to charge ahead. That there were no vorgs or wielders of magic among the ranks of the enemy his warriors laid waste to on this battlefield surprised Galad. Vorgs made up the bulk of Kragan's army. The wielder was obviously sacrificing his conscripts in a mass attack into the haze, filling Galad with a growing sense of unease.

What purpose was he failing to divine within this carnage?

When the mists stopped flowing, seeming to freeze in place, Galad felt as if a swarm of ants had crawled up his spine. There could be only one reason behind the enemy's ploy: Laikas was in trouble.

Galad signaled the retreat and crossed into another of the rychly mists, repeating the pattern until he knew time sped his steps to a dozen times normal. The winding, sunlit path between the other time-mists led him up the steep slope between the thick trunks of blue spruce. As he approached the murky barriers that surrounded the glade where Laikas had stationed herself, he slowed almost to a stop, gradually forcing himself through the resistance of the slowing vapors that reduced the passage of time. And as he emerged into each of these new regions, the fog melted away to again bathe his body in sunlight, even as the mists closed in behind him.

Always leading with his head and arms, he readied himself for the surprising dangers these new zones could bring. But instead of danger, he found death. Laikas lay in the middle of the glade, surrounded by the unmoving wisps. Blood from the jagged hole where her throat had once been covered her uniform and pooled around her body, matting her hair. Her eyes stared out of a face locked in an expression he at first took for terror. But as he knelt to take her hand in his, Galad was shocked to see that her face shone with passion such as he had only seen during their lovemaking.

Feeling a tremble make its way from his hand into the rest of his body, Galad blinked away tears, raised her fingers to his lips, and gently kissed them as his warriors spread out around the glade to defend it. No attack came.

When Galad released her hand to slowly rise to his feet, he turned to the warrior who stood at his side. Captain Tempas, his second-in-command, was easily recognizable by the much lighter skin of the scar that carved a path from her hairline across the bridge of her nose. At ninety-three, she was just entering middle age but had proven herself his most adept mist warrior and a charismatic leader. Despite her knowledge that this death meant that the mists Laikas had created would shortly fade away, Tempas's eyes held only sympathy for his loss.

With a shuddering breath, Galad forced himself to focus on the danger that now confronted them all.

"Send runners to all of my commanders. Have them tell of the death of Laikas and that I have ordered the retreat to our rally point. Then assign a warrior to carry her body. As soon as you have completed that task, we move. We must be far from here before the mists dissipate."

Slapping palm to fist in salute, Tempas turned and strode away.

With one last look at his fallen lover, Galad allowed fury to shunt aside his grief. Then he shifted his gaze to the tale that the ground told him. A furrow where rock and soil had been pushed aside to form a mound where none had previously existed could mean only one thing. Elemental magic of the earthen variety had been at work here. He could smell the evil taint of it on the mountain air.

Galad wanted to charge into his enemies, cutting a swath all the way to Kragan, sure that only the ancient one who had assumed a primordial's form could have done this. No other could have overcome Laikas so easily. But with no time-shaper to support his assault, Galad would only be sacrificing his mist warriors for vengeance.

So as grief robbed the strength from his limbs, Galad led his followers along mist-shrouded pathways higher into the Glacier Mountains.

17

Areana's Vale
YOR 415, Mid-Spring

If he had thought about it, Newton realized, he would have never come on this misbegotten, ill-thought-out adventure that was soon going to get him killed. He would have made his way to Hannington instead of journeying far from the comforts of Tal.

Now his panic attack on the cliffs had gotten him scorned, even by his own family. Everyone blamed him for what had happened to Corporal Jones, almost as if he had intended to get Jonesy killed.

It wasn't even his fault. They had all known that he was terrified of heights before they had ordered him up on those cliffs. Hadn't he told them? Wasn't it blatantly obvious? And hadn't he tried to overcome his fears with an effort that enabled him to climb that terrible trail for some three hundred feet before he had slipped? Little wonder that panic had overcome him as death tugged at his ankles.

And so he stood here in the darkness, the drums hammering at the canyon walls as if to pull them down onto all those who waited. Newton was more scared now than he had been while dangling from that rock high above. If circumstances had allowed him the opportunity to eat earlier in the day, Newton was quite certain he would be puking it out here and now onto these other poor fellows who waited in the night beside him.

So he endured the endless wait as lightning crackled overhead. Archers on both sides exchanged volleys, and on the fortress walls above, men battled to keep vorgs from clambering up ramps and ladders. Soldiers cried out and fell, some silently, others calling for their wives or mothers as their lifeblood leached away. A loud crash sounded at the drawbridge, and men rushed forward to brace it but were flung aside by a terrible blow that shook the earth, throwing Newton and all those near him to the ground.

As he struggled to regain his feet, someone stumbled into Newton. To his utter horror, lightning lit the compound, revealing that the man had no face left. It had been gouged, ripped, or bitten from his head, leaving only a ghastly wet and dripping surface of bone and teeth through which a lolling tongue appeared.

Newton scrambled away from the terrible apparition, skinning hands and knees on the ground as he struggled to get free. Reaching his feet, he ran like he had never run before, ducking back along the narrow winding road packed with soldiers waiting for the fight to come to them.

Everywhere angry yells and reaching hands clutched at him, attempting to throw him back into the fight or perhaps to kill him themselves, but with a strength born of madness, he eluded them. Onward his headlong flight took him, across one drawbridge after another, startling and angering those he passed, but he never succumbed to their efforts to stop him.

Passing out of the canyon into the western edge of Areana's Vale, he glanced upward, a desperate idea taking hold in his brain. There was one safe place that would not fall.

Crazy Carol, on her outcropping high above, would not succumb to the battle that raged below. She had already proven that she could shield herself and the Endarian from the attacks of the priests.

If he could get up there with her, surely she would take pity on him and allow him the protection of the ledge. She had once been kind to him. Yes, she would remember and take pity.

In the storm-lit darkness, Newton scrambled up the narrow path as fast as his arms and legs could propel him, all thoughts of his fear of heights lost to a past where reason reigned instead of madness.

—⚬⚬—

Inside the protective bubble that she kept in place as a shield against the persistent assaults of the priests, a cool night breeze swirled Carol's cloak about her. She reached outward with her mind, tracing backward along the energies that attacked her, putting imaginary pins in a mental map that plotted their positions.

Once she individually identified protectors, she tagged the signatures of their minds and touched them ever so softly with her own, too gently for them to notice but enough that she could find any that she so touched. So far she had identified thirty-three of them, twenty-seven of whom remained alive.

Some lashed out at her, while a few others attempted to attack the forts below. All these she blocked, sending out occasional probing attacks of her own. It broke her heart that good men were dying atop the walls far below, men whom she could save if she swept these vorgs and their priests from the canyon. But the canyon was long, the entire length of it jammed with her enemies.

Beyond the lower end, many thousands more clamored for their chance to attack, their thirst for blood thwarted for the moment by the narrow ravine that only allowed a small percentage of their number entrance. Among those thousands outside the canyon, many more of the priests waited, making judgments about her strength from her actions.

They wanted her exhausted, both from the physical drain of staying awake and from the battle she waged against their lead elements. They would not want to commit the bulk of their magical forces until they had convinced themselves that she was at the brink of collapse.

Carol was indeed tired. Fighting, by its very nature, even when engaging lesser foes, was draining, and in this case she was fighting in a manner designed to entice more of her enemies to give themselves away. The fact that they had not yet responded by increasing the numbers against her meant that they weren't falling for the trap. Either that, or they had some other plan that they were trying to mask. The only reason she was not even more tired sat beside her.

Kim pulled energy from her surroundings with abilities that only some Endarians possessed. Because of the special mental link that existed between the half sisters, she was able to funnel that energy to Carol far more easily than she could when otherwise practicing her healing arts.

Because of their bond, Carol knew that Kim was frustrated and fearful. Kim feared for John and wanted badly to be down below helping tend to the wounded, to be near her husband as he fought. Down there, Kim would be close enough to the fighting to use the portion of her abilities that she had always shunned—the ability to transfer wounds from friendly soldiers to their enemies as they fought.

Instead, Kim chose to funnel the scant natural life energy available in nearby plants that grew inside crevices within the stone into Carol, helping to keep her from collapsing. Carol could feel all these things within her sister, feelings that brought forth her own darker fears. Where was Arn? She angrily pushed that worry from her consciousness.

If her father had not given her specific instructions to save her strength to support the khan's counterattack, she could not have resisted involving herself in the fight that now raged inside the lowest of the river forts. As it was, she had felt it necessary to strike down the giant gruns, an act that had not kept the vorgs from breaching the drawbridge.

She had attempted to search out the minds of the priests using the skills that she had learned these last months, but to no avail. There were so many tormented, twisted souls crammed into the valley that connecting with each mind was impossible.

But that was not the case when protectors brought themselves to her attention by using their magic. Once she identified them, she did not lose sight of them. In her mind, they glowed, filthy beacons in a sea of darkness. The protectors who remained outside the gorge must believe she was having great difficulty dealing with the twenty-seven that remained alive within it.

Carol had sewn together her early warning system using a patchwork of minor elementals whose only purpose was to alert her if any spell was cast against her position or the fortress below. Her ability to monitor the protectors that she had already identified and mentally tagged rendered these precautions moot except when additional priests entered the fray from beyond the fortress walls. But these were the steps she hoped would provide her a critical advantage when the protectors decided to conduct an all-out attack.

Carol's defensive bubble only existed as an optical illusion. When the priests struck out at her, a small cadre of elementals under direct control diverted the energy of the attacks away from her or in some cases away from the fortress below, leading to the visual effect of the fireballs and lightning striking the surface of an invisible shield along which they crawled.

There were only a few ways to overcome such a defense magically. One was to cast an attack spell stronger than the powers of the elementals controlled by the defender. Another was to take control of the opposing wielder's elementals. Yet another approach was to overwhelm the defender with so many different forms of attacks that some got through.

Some of the protectors wielded elementals using defensive mechanisms similar to those that Carol employed, while others attacked. She could feel the putrid essence of their minds as they worked to gain control of stronger elemental forces to launch against her.

"Carol!"

The call diverted her attention to the path leading to the ledge where she stood beside Kim. To her surprise, Jaradin Scot stood several feet down the trail that led to her outcropping, gesturing toward her.

"I have a message from High Lord Rafel," he called.

"What is it?"

"He said it is for your ears only," Jaradin yelled, motioning toward Kim.

"What can be said to me can be said in front of Kim."

She noticed that Jaradin was having a hard time hearing her as the thunder rumbled overhead. Upon the ledge, Carol had muted the sound, but Jaradin was not yet within her protected radius. The noise where he stood must be nearly deafening.

"I know, but those were my instructions. May I come up?"

Carol marveled, as she had often done in the past, at the way men tended to take her father's orders so literally that all reason vanished. Better to just let them accomplish their task and be on their way than to try to reapply reason that was so thoroughly missing.

"Come ahead," she said, returning her attention to search for any hint of new threats.

A new voice startled her. "No! Save me, not him!"

A young soldier plunged onto the ledge, eyes wide, almost rolling within their sockets. His shoulder struck the surprised ranger as the newcomer struggled to get near Carol. The glancing blow knocked a dagger from Jaradin's hand, sending it skittering off the edge of the pinnacle to disappear into the darkness below.

What stunned her, though, was the insane fury etched into Jaradin's scarred face, a look that had been directed at her before the soldier had collided with him. The ranger reacted violently, grabbing the youth and flipping him onto the ground. Before the stunned Carol could react, he delivered a vicious kick to the lad's midsection. The soldier rolled backward, scrabbled at the edge for an instant, and then, with a scream, plummeted outward and down.

As Jaradin spun back toward Carol, Kim leapt at him, a dagger of elegant design appearing in her hand as if she had plucked it from the air. Jaradin gestured, and Kim slumped to the ground.

A new maleficent light appeared in Carol's mind, the signature of a powerful wielder casting a spell very close to her. As the force of Jaradin's magic struck at her, she lashed out, catching the assaulting elemental just as it reached her. The being tore at her with invisible claws, opening a two-inch cut along her left forearm, just below the elbow.

Then she had it. Encased in the crushing grip of her will, the air elemental Vejas howled in misery and frustration. Around the ledge, the protective shield that Ohk held in place wavered, allowing the outside attacks to press farther inward.

She tossed Vejas away in disgust as she reestablished her hold on Ohk, restoring her protective shielding. Her mind shifted its focus to the one who stood before her. The grin on Jaradin's face melted away. He struggled to rush toward her but could no longer move.

Carol could feel the evil that emanated from the man's being as she probed the surface of his mind, thrusting deeper within, barging through the mental barriers he attempted to erect in her way. What she found was not Jaradin Scot but a shadowy priest who thought of himself as Angloc, a beast whose disgusting desires sent her into a killing rage.

She worked her way deeper into the priest's being, imprisoning his spirit and taking control of his body. With a thought, she forced him to walk toward the ledge, stopping when he balanced precariously on the precipice. One more step, and he would go to the death he deserved.

A faint whisper in his mind stopped her. What was that? It felt so different, so full of heart. Carol probed deeper, ignoring the efforts of the immobilized priest, seeking that small light that must be what remained of the real Jaradin Scot.

Like a tracker interpreting the turned twigs in a dim trail, Carol followed the traces of Jaradin outward, beyond his body, the ethereal trace coming to a stop in a lightless place far away, where a man she did not recognize sat in a damp cell. Within that fragile body, the bright soul of Jaradin Scot shone forth.

"I am here; do not be alarmed," Carol whispered across the void.

The body in the cell stiffened in alarm.

"Jaradin, I need you to trust me. I need you to know that I am real and not a figment of your imagination. Can you do that for me?"

"I can," Jaradin said aloud in his small prison. Even the mental projection of the voice sounded dry, accompanied by a weak croak of a laugh. "My imagination doesn't talk that way."

Carol strengthened the pathway between them. "Jaradin, I'm going to try to reverse what the priests did to you, swapping your mind back to your own body and sending the priest's back to his. Be ready."

"Have been for a long while now."

She reached deeply into the minds of the two men, finding the place where each had a small anchor back to his physical self. Slowly she set to work increasing the strength of that natural bond, keeping both ends in balance.

Suddenly there was a snap, the force of which broke Carol's hold upon their minds, sending her to one knee on the high ledge, almost causing her to lose her connection to the shielding around the pinnacle. Once again, the bubble wavered, the white light within dimming to a fraction of its former glory.

This time the restoration of the protective barrier took longer, and she was horrified to discover just how much the effort of the mind transfer had drained her. She had allowed herself to lose sight of the critical mission at hand in order to save one man, possibly dooming them all.

She glanced down at Jaradin's prostrate body lying next to Kim's and received another shock: her sister was unconscious.

Now Carol stood truly alone, having exhausted herself for a small purpose and with no one left to help her recover her strength. She touched Kim's mind gently with her own and, then, satisfied that her sister would live, straightened to stand proud once more.

An icy blast spiked outward from her outstretched arms, freezing one of the priests where he stood, a quarter league from her spire. At that moment the first ray of dawn shone through a crack in the blanket of night overhead. A rush of clouds boiled into the narrow gap like the maw of some great beast snapping shut on its prey. Dawn found the canyon no brighter than before.

—⁓—

Far away in a filthy cell, a lone figure screamed.

PART III

I have lived the cursed existence of a life-shifter, stealing that which is most precious from living things that I may gift it to others. That I have stolen the life essence from intelligent beings haunts my days and nights.

—From the *Scroll of Landrel*

18

Gorloch was not happy. Every vorg that Jorthain had placed under his command had a reputation, ruthless killers all. As far as he was concerned, though, they bitched and moaned like human weaklings. He ran at the head of the storm column, a term used among vorgs for their special units, and every time he looked back, some of the warriors were lagging. He slowed the pace slightly, although doing so infuriated him.

They were still several marches away from their quarry, and at this rate, with the amount of rest stops these so-called elite hunters were requiring, it would take two full days to find the man and kill him. True, that timeline was still a full week ahead of the schedule that Jorthain had given him to accomplish the task, but it was hardly satisfactory to the leader of the storm column.

Then there was the annoying fact that he had periodically sighted a lone horseman, clad in black and riding a black horse, trailing along behind them in the distance. The fellow made no effort to hide the fact that he was tailing them but kept his distance, only allowing for an occasional glimpse against the horizon. Gorloch did not like being followed. He did not like being watched. And he sure did not like having no idea who was doing so.

But the stranger was no threat, and Gorloch would brook no delays to go hunt down the insolent fool. More than likely he was one of Jorthain's spies, keeping tabs on their progress. It didn't matter. Gorloch would deal with him after he finished the mission.

The sky flared red as the sun sank behind the horizon in the west, then faded to a purple haze as the evening crept in. Gorloch stopped, holding his fist high.

"Rest break. You have three hours. Don't make me wake you. Jarsh, you and Frolth have guard duty."

The two stepped forward, their anger apparent in their bared fangs.

"Guard duty?" asked Jarsh, the larger one. "Frolth and I need a little rest, too."

The other vorg nodded his head. "By the deep, we do."

Gorloch grabbed each of the two by the throat and lifted them off the ground. "Listen to me, you motherless sons of whores. One more complaint, and I'll give you an eternity of rest. Do you understand me?"

Interpreting their gagging sounds as agreement, Gorloch tossed the vorgs away from him, sending them rolling across the ground to the considerable amusement of the others. Gorloch turned on the rest of them. "Now you have less than three hours to rest."

The vorgs met that pronouncement by slumping down on the ground in as comfortable a spot as they could find. Sleep was a luxury Gorloch would not allow himself until he completed his mission, one of the reasons that he was rapidly becoming the most feared of the high vorg guard to Jorthain. He had no doubt that he would soon rise to general of the army of the protectors, displacing that incompetent General Jerg. How that idiot had been selected to lead the army was a mystery that did not speak well of their high priest master.

Gorloch shoved the thoughts of his ambition aside. It would do him little good to brood. Focus on the mission. That was the key.

He strode away from the camp, his senses keen in the dark. Out there, in front of them, was a man that Jorthain wanted dead. To send out a storm column to kill a single rider while the army moved against the witch of the mountains was mystifying. But since Jorthain wanted him killed, Gorloch would make sure it happened, although he did not expect Jorthain's rider to survive to report the success back to his master.

The rest break passed with him finding nothing out of the ordinary at either of the guard posts. Both vorgs were alert and ready, despite their earlier recalcitrance. Nodding his approval to each in turn, Gorloch slowly circled the camp.

As the rest break drew to a close, he made his way back to camp. Already the band of vorg hunters had begun to assemble, which he noted with some satisfaction. Given enough time, he would teach this rabble what it was like to be elite.

As Jarsh and Frolth reappeared from their guard posts, he counted those assembled. His mood soured. Fifteen, including himself. Five were still sleeping. Leaving the others in formation, he stormed back to the sleeping area, fulsome in his knowledge that it would be some time before they would dare to sleep anywhere near him again.

The sense of wrongness hit him as he approached the first of the sleepers, who lay separately along the north edge of the camp. Gorloch paused, sniffing the night air, which suddenly seemed to hang heavy with portent. The breeze was from the south and held only traces of the rest of the vorg encampment—rotting meat that they had pulled from packs to eat before sleep, excrement and urine in the wood line, but nothing else.

All that changed as he kicked the first of the sleeping vorgs so hard that the body rolled two feet. The stench of vorg blood swept up to his nostrils as his eyes took in the scene. He bent down. The warrior lay in a large pool of blood, his neck cut so neatly that he never had time to awake fully enough to know that he was dead. Moving rapidly among the other bodies, Gorloch found the same thing: vorgs killed quickly and silently in their sleep, unaware of the darkness that crept over them.

With a bellow of rage, he ran back to the spot where his hunters awaited. So the black rider was not one of Jorthain's. Little matter. He had merely earned himself an earlier death than Gorloch had been planning for him. The man was an assassin, a fact that did nothing but whet Gorloch's appetite. He had no particular respect for the breed, being mostly made up of folk too timid to come at you unless you slept. Well, his vorgs slept no longer, something that the killer was about to find out.

"It seems we can no longer ignore the rider on our trail. Jarsh, Frolth, and you, Lraarog, I want you to pick up his track and hurry. The man is an assassin, so enjoy yourselves with him. He can't have more than about an hour's lead on you. I want his head in this sack when you get back."

Gorloch tossed a burlap bag at Frolth.

"We will not wait for you, so hustle back along our trail as soon as you've killed him. A hundred gold bonus to each of you as soon as you hand that bag back to me."

With a growl of approval and anticipation, the three battle vorgs raced northward through the darkness.

Once again, Gorloch led his warriors forward at a run, settling on a pace that could be maintained indefinitely in preference to the faster, shorter bursts at which they had been traveling. He did not intend to stop again until the next nightfall, and then only for a short food and water stop. With any luck, the three hunters he had sent after the assassin would link back up then.

The paying out of bounty money was not something that Gorloch liked to do, feeling that it established a bad precedent, but this case begged for him to make an exception. He was only sorry that he could not personally take the time to tear the mysterious rider's head from his shoulders and suck the marrow from his spine.

By late in the day, the vorgs of the storm column caught sight of the original target. He was across a broad valley, cresting a ridge several leagues to the south of their position, and he clearly also saw them. The sight cheered Gorloch greatly since the rider's bay horse was noticeably exhausted, barely able to keep up a shambling trot. The kill would come by tomorrow afternoon.

The evening rest break came and went quickly, with no sign of the three vorgs he had sent after the assassin. No matter. They would just have to catch up as best they could if they wanted their bounty. Gorloch was in no mood to wait for them, rousting his unit into motion as soon as they had finished eating a ration of the meat they carried with them, washing the stinking flesh down with the liquid in their waterskins.

Normally the darkness before dawn was a time that Gorloch liked, the blackness enhanced by the thought of the coming light of day. Such was not the case in the hours before this dawn. The first of his men to become horribly ill was Grollg, perhaps the best of his hunters and the only one of the current group whom he had taken with him on a previous mission. One moment they were jogging through the wooded hills, and the next Grollg was spewing his life essence out through every orifice of his body.

The vorg fell to his knees, hurling vomit with such force that it splattered all those nearby, the recipients of the splatter recoiling backward as much from the smell as from the splattering of bile that hit them. And it was not just bile. The scent of blood was heavy in the air, although that was almost immediately overtaken by the foul odor of Grollg's bowels.

As Gorloch moved toward him, another of his vorgs doubled over, doing his best to imitate the scene created by Grollg. This one was followed almost immediately by two more vorgs performing the same intestinal acrobatics. The stench of blood, feces, urine, and bile filled the air around the sick vorgs, sending most of their comrades backing away. Gorloch moved rapidly from one of the ailing vorgs to another as they howled in pain between bouts of vomiting. Within ten minutes, all four lay dead on the trail.

"Poisoned!"

The murmur from the vorgs grew into a clamor of shouts. The assassin had poisoned their food and then slit the throats of the five vorgs. The deadly food had lain there in their packs until they had partaken at the recent rest stop.

"He's poisoned our food!" a vorg yelled.

"How do we know it was the food and not the water?" yelled another.

"I'm dumping it all!" a third shouted. "I'm not dying like that!"

Gorloch stepped into their midst, shoving the last speaker hard enough to send him tumbling to the ground. "Dump it if you want to, idiot bastards. If the assassin had poisoned your food and water, you would already be lying there beside those others. Quit squealing like a bunch of newborn piglets and get back in formation. As soon as the others get back from their hunt, we'll kick the black rider's head around among us until we tire of the game. In the meantime, let's move."

But even as he spoke the words, a dull ache of foreboding pounded his temples at the thought of the assassin and his tactics.

Having returned to a ground-burning jog, Gorloch's mood lifted as he felt the lust for the upcoming kill creep into those whom he led. He guessed they were less than four hours behind their quarry at this point, and there was nothing better for setting one's spirit right than to maim an enemy. There was no doubt that they would take their time with this one.

Rounding a bend in the trail, the storm column came to an abrupt halt as the first light of dawn spread a rosy glow across the eastern sky, lighting the open valley floor before them. In the midst of a wide clearing, the naked limbs of a giant cottonwood tree spread toward the sky like the claws of a great beast. From one of those limbs, feet up and head down, hung three forms, arms dangling toward the ground as if they were trying to grab for something they had dropped but could not quite reach.

As Gorloch made his way to that tree, it became obvious what they were reaching toward. Below the bodies of each of the vorgs he had sent after the black rider was a pile. The assassin had slit open their stomachs. He had hung them from a tree, then bled and gutted them as a hunter would do to his prey. He had delivered a message intended to make the entire storm column question who was the hunter and who the hunted.

Rage exploded through Gorloch with such force that it seemed his blood would spurt from his temples in pulsing streams. He wheeled back around to face the stunned remainder of his vorgs.

"Get back in formation."

"To the deep with you," sneered a vorg to his left, curved sword already in hand.

"Yeah, Gorloch. We're leaving, and there's nothing you can do to stop us," said another off to his right.

The battle captain erupted with such violence that the first of the rebellious vorgs died from the force of the blow from a closed left fist, bits of skull spinning off into clear morning air. Seeing the devastation of the blow, the second vorg turned to run, making it exactly thirteen steps before Gorloch's war hammer rained upon him, splattering his remains to the ground in a stew.

Gorloch spun toward the remaining five vorgs. "Any more complaints?"

To no one's surprise, there were not.

As they began running forward in formation once again, Gorloch caught sight of a lone rider in black sitting on his horse atop the ridgeline to their east, less than a half league away. Though every fiber of his being screamed for vengeance, he ignored the feeling, letting the mission drive him forward. The rider's death would come soon enough, and he, Gorloch, would be the reaper.

Within an hour, the storm column crossed the trail left by the man they had first been sent to kill, a track clear enough that anyone could follow. To someone of Gorloch's skill, it might as well have been made by a train of wagons, yet he paused momentarily to examine the spoor. The regularity with which small rocks were overturned or knocked from their resting places indicated the exhaustion of the man's mount. At this point it was practically dragging its hooves along the top of the earth.

The trail turned through a small rough ravine, the sides of which were steep, but not so steep that a horse could not climb, although the sharp branches of the juniper trees and scrub bushes that covered the rocky slopes would have made such passage uncomfortable. Their quarry had kept to the streambed rather than fight the rougher terrain. So much the better; it merely meant that Gorloch and his vorgs could move faster.

Whether it was the hint of a different man-scent on the breeze or a distant sound behind him, Gorloch was not sure, but something brought him to a halt, and he looked back along the trail behind him. As the last of his hunters rounded the bend, a rock the size of a melon crashed down from above, caving in the side of the vorg's head, followed by a flurry of sliding gravel. The sound of running feet sped away through the thick brush higher on the steep slope above.

The vorgs of his column raced after the sound.

"Do not chase that man!"

Gorloch's bellow brought the two nearest troops to a stop, but the other two had already disappeared around the bend.

The captain was beside himself with rage. The idiots were racing into a prepared trap, of that he had no doubt, nor did he have any doubt as to the outcome. Turning on the remaining two hunters of his column, he grabbed them by their shoulders, practically throwing them down the trail ahead.

"Stay on mission. Never let your enemy set your direction. If you so much as get out of my shadow, I will kill you myself."

Gorloch upped the pace. Another hour, maybe two, was all he needed to catch their target, and then he would turn his attention to the assassin. He had altered his assessment of the black rider's abilities—the man was far better than he would have imagined—but in the end it would make no difference. He had made a mistake in bringing himself to Gorloch's attention, a mistake that dozens before him had made, much to their detriment.

The sun had risen nearly to its zenith when the ravine broadened out suddenly, spreading out into an open valley with a single hill in its center. Atop that rise, the soldier that they hunted stood beside the body of his horse, having run the animal to its death. He appeared to be a boy no more than sixteen years of age.

A grin split Gorloch's face as he burst from the wood line, a grin that departed as a black figure stepped from the trees thirty feet to his right, halting him and the two remaining members of his storm column in their tracks.

As if in slow motion, the vorgs to his left side both raised their bows, thick shafts drawing back as they elevated. Twin glimmers of whirling steel appeared in the assassin's hands, darting across the intervening space before the bows finished their rise.

The shafts of the daggers pierced the throats of his two vorgs, and as their bodies acquired a sudden limpness, their arrows arced harmlessly out and away.

The assassin stepped toward Gorloch, a new blade that exuded an unnatural lack of light now in his hand.

"I don't think you're going to harm that lad."

With a snarl Gorloch charged, swinging his war hammer into the assassin with such force that the wind howled around the head of the weapon. As it crashed down toward its target, the assassin moved so swiftly that his image blurred within Gorloch's vision.

Gorloch staggered past the man in black, whirling for his next attack. Odd. Now everything seemed a bit blurry, and the hammer felt slippery in his hand. Glancing down, he stared in amazement. Where was all that blood coming from?

As his vision contracted to a funnel and the ground rushed up to his face, the answer came.

19

Glacier Mountains, Southeast of Endar
YOR 415, Mid-Spring

Fate had driven Galad to this decision. For his entire adult life, he had refused his mother's urgings that he embrace the natural ability that destiny had bestowed upon him. But now, the lives of those under his command hung in the balance.

Under his command.

For one last time, he gazed upon the thousand surviving mist warriors as their commander, struggling to keep his hands from shaking. This ceremony would put an end to his role.

Galad stepped forward to the spot where Captain Tempas stood at the front of the brigade. Like the warriors behind her, she stood at attention, her long hair hanging over the shoulders of her color-shifting uniform. When Galad stopped in front of her, Tempas clapped her left palm to right fist in salute, a movement that he echoed. When she returned to attention, Galad swallowed, then raised his voice so that it echoed from the forested ridges that formed the sides of this grassy valley.

"Captain Tempas, I hereby transfer to you the rank and title of commander. Since I must take on the role of time-shaper, my brigade is now yours."

The two exchanged one more salute before Commander Tempas turned to face her warriors. His mouth suddenly as dry as the Mogev Desert, Galad turned and walked away from his life as a mist warrior.

—⚏—

Galad needed more time to practice channeling and controlling the time-mists if he was to approach the skills that Laikas had mastered. So, having informed Commander Tempas that he intended to be gone just a few days, Galad departed, carrying with him several weeks of travel rations. Because of the location he had selected, water would not be an issue. There was a reason these mountains were named after the glaciers that crawled through the high country.

Once he was well beyond the valley guarded by Tempas's mist-warrior brigade, Galad stepped out into a glacier-filled canyon and set down his pack and his bow. Bowing his head in concentration, he knelt and reached out with his left hand toward the surface. He did not touch the ice but instead began tracing a pace-thick cube above it. As he did so, he channeled the flow of time into that hand and out through his right, which he pointed along the glacier to the northeast.

At first he pulled gently, slowing time within the cube he built of the pomaly mist, accelerating time within the outflowing river of rychly mist. Although it had been a long while since he had last practiced the technique, his mother had forced him to undergo years of training in the craft before he had come of age to set his own path. In his mind, he could still hear the mellifluous voice of his favorite teacher, Diena, as she cautioned him about the dangers of the craft.

Any attempt to channel more time than a shaper's talent allows will result in her or his death. You, young Galad, must explore your limits carefully. No one else can do that for you.

Galad had never tried to determine what the limits on his ability to channel the mists of time might be. He was now determined to remedy that shortcoming.

Ever so gradually, he increased the scope of his channel, further slowing time within the cube as he spread and layered the rychly mists that flowed out from his extended arm, visualizing the familiar terrain across which speed now flowed. Three items had to be balanced in order to create the mists: the size of each fog, its duration, and its intensity.

Eventually satisfied with what he had done, Galad dismissed his channel. As he did so, the river of mists ceased flowing, becoming an unmoving bank of fog many leagues in length. To those who remained outside the rychly zones, the mists would dissipate within a few days. Still kneeling, he ran his hand along the milky-white surface of the cube. Within it, time passed so slowly that it felt solid to the touch. The tip of an arrow fired at the area would slowly penetrate, but the momentum of all that remained outside the zone would force the shaft to deflect or break. And the pomaly mist that formed the block would not dissipate for decades.

Galad rose to his feet and slung his pack and bow over his shoulders. Then he stepped into the first layer of the rychly fogbank.

To his eyes, it was as if he had not entered a mist, time's rate of change seemingly unaffected. But another fog merged behind him. For several strides, the path remained clear. Then he encountered the next rychly layer, knowing that, within, time accelerated again. He needed to create these gradual transitions in order to make passage between the mists possible. Again and again he transitioned, feeling as if he was fighting his way out of the mud.

When he made the final passage, a vast stretch of the glacier opened out before him. He knew that he was now in the fastest changing rychly mist, but to him it felt like a region of normality. The sun was in the western sky, whereas he had first stepped into the mists during the morning. The sight of the sinking sun pulled forth the memory of a time when he had sat lakeside, his arm around Laikas's soft shoulders as they both awaited the sunset. She had smelled of honey-berry leaves and lavender; she was a much wiser and kinder soul than he would ever be. An ache spread through his torso, pulling Galad back to the present. He was surprised to find his arms wrapped around his gut, as if to hold in his organs. Angry, he shoved such thoughts of weakness aside. He would mourn later.

Galad walked farther out onto the brilliant white surface of the ice and made camp. For the next several weeks, this is where he would train. Here he would age at many times the rate of those he had left behind. To them, he would only be gone a couple of days.

Using his sword, Galad carved out a chunk of ice and put it in a metal pot. He removed the focus-glass from his pack and propped it against the side of the pot such that it bent the sun's rays inward, forming a hot spot on the ice within. Taking out a strip of dried meat, he set it inside the pot and settled back to wait. After he assuaged his hunger and thirst, he would begin the task he had set for himself.

20

Areana's Vale
YOR 415, Mid-Spring

The crimson light of dawn glinted like blood from the crescent ax blades of the three thousand horsemen. They sat in formation, hidden by the ragged crest of the ridgeline from the vorgs who spilled across the broad valley beyond. White puffs of mist bloomed from the nostrils of the horses in the cold morning air. The khan's steed carried him along the lines of men, his right arm raised palm outward in acknowledgment of every warrior who sat astride their mounts, the traditional salute to those who were about to fight and die for their khan.

The khan's ax called to him as he sat atop the stallion, urging him to turn and lead the charge so that it might sate its bloodthirst. But the beast would have to wait. His warriors would get their due, each one of them, a direct look into the eyes of their khan and his personal salute. In a short while he would lead these men over that ridge and into battle, but first he would share the bond of brotherhood with them.

Having finished his circuit, the khan rode up the hillside at the front of his warriors, thirty-three companies of the finest riders in the world. There were no bridles on their mounts. Each horse had been trained to the leg, leaving both hands free for battle. The only killers that could compare to his men and their mounts were the fabled centaurs. But as the vorgs beyond the ridge were about to find out, his horsemen were no fable. The khan raised his ax high and then hung it from its strap at the pommel of his saddle, unlimbering his short bow as he did. His thirty-three hundred men repeated his actions in unison. Only Ty failed to follow suit, sitting with his ax resting across his legs.

The khan's steed spun and picked up a trot toward the crest above. Behind him the companies fell in three riders abreast, a great snake uncoiling and slithering forth in search of prey. The khan increased his speed to an easy canter as he crested the ridge, the great triple column of riders behind him matching his pace as the line began to stretch out.

The sky had become a blazing orange glow that illuminated the massive army stretched across the broad valley to his south, a force made up mostly of vorgs but also large numbers of bandits, marauders, and other foul things pulled from the nether regions of the earth. The horde milled about, jammed against the narrow rent in the cliffs to the east, the mighty canyon that led upward to Areana's Vale. The army of the protectors churned in disorder as the companies of the host pushed at one another to gain entrance. None wanted to miss being present for the pillage that would follow the slaughter of Rafel's force.

The leading tip of the khan's spearhead had crossed half the distance that separated them from the army of the protectors before the vorgs noticed them. A great hue and cry arose as the surprised vorgs turned to meet them. A quarter of a league ahead, a hastily erected pike line tilted into place to meet the horsemen's charge. Black clouds boiled into the sky to blot out the morning sun, hurled upward by a group of priests who gathered atop a distant knoll.

"Okay, Rafel," Khan muttered as he urged his stallion to a gallop, "I guess we're about to find out if that daughter of yours is as good as you say."

The horses in the long line that snaked across the valley behind the khan matched him stride for stride.

Along the base of the clouds, lightning gathered, multiple forks striking toward the horsemen. The air above their heads shimmered like ripples rising above hot desert sands. Along this, the lightning crawled, unable to reach its targets on the ground below. Blasts of thunder smote at them, only to be drowned out by the thunder of hooves that pounded toward their enemies. Lord Alan's claims of his sister's magic-wielding prowess had not been overstated.

By the time the khan was within a hundred paces of the waiting vorgs, twenty-foot pikes bristled like the back of a giant porcupine. As he bore down on the horse impalers, he laughed.

At fifty paces, the khan whirled his horse into a hard right turn, loosing three arrows in quick succession from his bow. Behind him the mighty snake struck. As each threesome of horsemen hit the turning point, each rider released a triplet of arrows into the pikemen, nine arrows per row. As they spun away after the khan, the next triplet released their arrows so that the flow of shafts looked like water squirting from the end of a pipe. Beside the khan, the bare-chested Kanjari kept pace, his golden locks blowing out behind him like the mane and tail of his palomino stallion.

The vorgs holding the pikes fell before the deadly stream in waves. Others attempting to rush forward to fill the gaps in the ranks met the same fate. And the snake writhed before them.

The khan maintained his gallop, leading those behind him in an arc away from the vorgish lines, the snake recoiling for its next strike. Slinging his bow, the khan hoisted his battle-ax, bringing his warhorse to a trot. The companies behind him gathered once more into broad lines, waiting for the tail end of their brothers to finish their rain of death.

The horde had been caught unprepared for a horse charge that invited pikemen to meet it, but now small groups of archers were beginning to fire into the khan's warriors. Although some of his men fell, the enemy could not get a clear line of sight past the pikemen, and thus the bulk of their quarrels went wide of the mark.

As the end of the line of riders neared the turning point, the khan swept his ax outward and down. Behind him, the bulk of his riders spread out and hurled themselves toward the ragged tear in the fabric of the waiting army. The khan's warriors struck en masse, trampling the bodies of the dead and dying as their axes struck and struck again. Ty, having moved to the fore, cut a swath through those that awaited, heading straight toward the gorge that led to Rafel's fortifications.

The khan's men merged with the army of the protectors, and their progress slowed. The initial shock of their attack subsided as the throng's great superiority in numbers began to assert itself. Forces that were not directly engaged by the horsemen began mounting counterattacks. An organized force of vorgs charged into the khan's right flank. Even though hundreds died beneath hoof and ax, they managed to separate several companies of his warriors from the main body.

The khan continued to lead the rest of his warriors toward his objective, unwilling to stop his forward momentum. Overhead, the magical shielding grew ragged as the confusion of the battle made it hard for Rafel's daughter to establish a cohesive defense. Bolts of lightning occasionally struck into their midst, killing both horsemen and those they fought.

As Khan closed to within a quarter of a league from the canyon entrance, a horror arose to his right front. From an obsidian portal, a nightmare figure stepped forward, multiple arms on each side raking outward with foot-long talons, its face a mass of curling teeth within a multiflapped central maw. The creature tore its way through the unfortunate vorgs that blocked its path toward the khan, shredding bodies and tossing the steaming mess aside. As it came, a low wail wept from its mouth.

A single word slipped from the khan's dry lips. "Slorg!"

—⚉—

A wave of dizziness assaulted Carol. Her difficulty in maintaining focus was getting to be a problem. For now, her shields were holding, both here and over the khan, but she felt her strength fading.

The part of her consciousness that scanned the field of minds for magical disturbances had lit up like a dried-out tree struck by lightning as the priests outside the canyon responded to the khan's attack. The initial shielding of the khan's forces had not been very difficult, but as the attack continued, more and more priests had joined in. So far she had identified one hundred and thirty-seven, most weak in sorcery. The sheer numbers began to weigh on her ability to concentrate, or perhaps she was simply fatigued. When the khan's forces separated into several groups, they compounded her difficulties.

Carol found it harder and harder to keep her mind focused on what she was doing. She began killing the priests, one or two at a time, but this drew another batch of new arrivals into the mystical fight, distracting her once again. Her mind drifted. Some of the attacks began to make it through or around her blocks. No, that wasn't it. For some reason she had momentarily dropped one of the shields, almost as if she had dozed off, waking herself as her head was about to nod forward.

Waves of exhaustion traveled through her limbs. She felt her knees shaking with weakness. Images of the soft mats and blankets of her bed slipped across her vision as a wave of cool numbness passed over her. It felt so good. If only she could rest for just a few seconds.

She glanced down at her body. That was funny. She could have sworn that she wore her white shirt. The left sleeve of this one was scarlet. Quite beautiful really, red fading to white as her eyes passed from left to right. She glanced at her left hand. A small rivulet of red ran slowly along her pink skin, dripping from the tips of her fingers in a slow trickle into a puddle of blood at her feet.

Her distant vulture's-eye view showed her a bolt of lightning that tore into the khan's men, bringing Carol out of her musings. With an effort, she focused, strengthening the shielding once again.

Suddenly she was aware of a new surge of magic and recognized it instantly from Hawthorne's old lessons. A summoning. It was madness to do such a thing. To allow a creature of the netherworld to cross over required that you give yourself to its control, allowing the demigod to take control of your body, distorting your living form to make room for its own.

Typically the summoned entity destroyed the mind of the host during the transfer. Hawthorne had said that some wielders attempted a deal with a primordial, offering up something that the entity wanted badly enough to allow the wielder to preserve his own mind, the two then sharing dominion over the body. It rarely worked out well for the wielder.

Even worse was to summon a slorg, a being so alien in mind that there was no hope of such an alliance. To summon one of those things allowed for only the transfer of a specific intent before the wielder succumbed to madness, and that intent became the beast's primal directive.

The intent could not be more complex than the mind of the thing the summoner called forth. Usually the directive revolved around hunger, hatred, or lust. What had just touched Carol's mind was one of the priests summoning such a creature.

Carol reached out to confront the abomination, but what she encountered sent her staggering backward. Unlike a person or an elemental, this thing had no thoughts. It didn't even have emotions, at least not in a way she could identify.

The slorg was merely a thing of appetite. Hunger consumed its flesh, a hunger to rend and kill. There was no turning its desire. It could not be dulled, and it could not be enhanced. This was a being that could only be sent back to its realm by waiting until after it sated its hunger. You could try to kill its host, but that host now bore all the strength and invulnerability of the slorg.

Once again Carol felt the inviting coolness move through her temples, passing through the nerves of her cheeks, sweeping like a soft brush down her throat, across the whole of her torso, her legs, her feet, leaving a tingle in her toes. It would be so nice to let go. To sink into that coolness. To let it take her away.

A deep sorrow descended on her as she sank to one knee. "Arn, where are you? I could really use a little help right now, my love."

A teardrop cut a trail from her left eye to the corner of her mouth. The salty taste added to her despair, opening a flood of tears that rushed down her face to drip from her chin into the pool of red in which she knelt. "I'm so sorry to have let you down."

The shielding around the pinnacle wavered, the light dimming almost to darkness.

A firm hand gripped her left arm just above the elbow, and a pair of arms enfolded Carol. Kim's face swam before her. She tilted a water pouch to Carol's mouth, and as the sorceress swallowed, the dizziness faded, and a wave of renewed strength flowed through her veins. The shielding resumed its former vigor.

"What in the world were you thinking?" Kim said as she helped Carol to her feet. "You almost let yourself bleed to death. If I hadn't awakened, you would have died, and everyone else would have perished along with you."

A weak smile creased the corners of Carol's mouth. "I got distracted."

"Next time, wake me. Stop worrying about me and just do it."

"Okay, big sister. I'll keep that in mind."

At Kim's touch the wound on her left arm slowed its bleeding. The vigor funneling into Carol through the Endarian acted as an elixir that, while unable to completely restore her strength, at least allowed her to regain focus.

Carol reached out with her mind toward the forces of the khan and the summoned thing that swept toward them. She hoped that she was not too late.

—᙭᙭—

Ty matched the khan as he turned at a right angle to the abomination that bore down on them, leading his warriors to carve a new path through the vorgs. With a gurgling roar, the slorg turned at an angle to intercept him, tearing its own trail of destruction through the protectors' army.

The vorgs and marauders fought to get out of the way of the monstrosity that ripped through their midst. Being pressed forward by the bulk of troops behind them and unable to run, they died by the dozens.

The khan increased his pace, cutting a swath through the vorgs. A yell of exaltation arose from his men, their great axes sweeping their foes aside as the hooves of their warhorses crushed foes underfoot. Bedlam reigned supreme as entire battalions of the opposing force panicked, rushing headlong into their own forces. Vorgs fleeing the slorg fought with vorgs trying to get to the khan. All the while, the paths of the horsemen and the slorg gradually converged.

Ty worked his ax with abandon, chopping through his enemies as he cleared the way forward. To his right, the khan's warhorse stumbled, pierced through the chest by the thick shaft of a vorgish pike. The stallion's front legs buckled, flipping the horse heels over head and hurling the khan into the crush of vorgs. Instantly they swarmed over him, chopping and hacking, sending up great gouts of blood and gore as they tore at the hated king of the horse people.

A magnificent shudder swept through the horsemen at the fall of their khan. Like the air going out of a punctured balloon, the attack faltered as a wave of depression and loss swept across their ranks. Into that malaise Ty thundered. He swept into the mass of vorgs that ripped at the body of the khan, his torso stretched taut as the great ax screamed through the air to rend those who stood before him. The vorgs cried out as Ty bore into them with a fury that caused them to forget about the slorg in deference to the bare-chested demon among them.

As he fought, Ty's laugh rang out across the field of battle, a sound of joy as pure as the clarion ring of church bells. And to that bell the horsemen rallied, racing to be close to him so that they might discover again this joy of battle that they had lost with the fall of their khan, only to find it reborn, burning hotter than ever in this vibrant god of war.

Ty's heart hammered in his chest. He cast his gaze across the horsemen, diminished in number now but fighting with a lust and vigor that would have brought tears of pride to the khan's eyes. If this were to be their end, then they would die in a manner that would gain them places of honor in the lands of the dead.

Carol's soft voice whispered in Ty's mind. "To the protectors."

Ty whirled his stallion around, gazing off to the west. There they were, gathered together on a hilltop less than a quarter league to the southwest. Dark-wall clouds swirled around the hill, lit from within by forks of lightning.

He brought his horse to a run in that direction, and the khan's warriors followed. He glanced back over his left shoulder. The slorg was closing the gap that separated them. The army of the protectors churned as if stirred by twin titans.

As the distance between himself and the protectors lessened, the fighting changed. The priests had kept their best troops close at hand, and these warriors fought to defend their masters as the protectors lashed out at the horsemen with magic. Although the shielding above Ty glowed white hot, it did not falter as it had a short time ago.

Two full battalions of armored vorgs counterattacked from the north, but several companies of riders turned automatically to meet that charge. Directly to the west, several thousand vorgs stood their ground, and their steadiness brought their fleeing brethren to a stop. These now turned to face the horsemen once again.

Ty glanced to his left, seeing that the slorg had closed to within a few hundred paces. Seeing that its target had slowed, the creature let forth a moan that ripped at the souls of all who heard it, sending chills down the spines of the strongest and sending the weak of spirit into spasms of fright. Its many arms whirled in a frenzy of motion that sent fountains of gore into the air as everything within its reach died violently.

"Almost there," Carol's voice whispered in his mind.

Not one of the khan's warriors faltered at the horrific sights and sounds. These horsemen would hold the line with him, whatever their fate, whatever the cost.

A lump rose in Ty's throat at the scene. Over a thousand horsemen, hair and beards stained with blood, battled astride their warhorses, axes rising and falling as they drove forward to help him avenge their khan.

These were men.

He faced forward once again, his blue eyes locked on the protectors. Okay. He would take their pet home to them.

—ᴡᴡ—

Carol's mind sailed across the battlefield, taking in the scene below from the perspective of the vulture, which a part of her now accompanied. A flock of the birds had gathered and now circled high above the fight that raged below, a feast that would fatten them for weeks to come.

On the floor of the valley, vorgs, human marauders, and the other rabble that made up the army of the protectors milled about in a maelstrom currently stirred by two giant spoons—the slorg and the glorious horsemen of the khan. Several small groups of the horsemen had become isolated from the main contingent, and although they still fought valiantly, they were being cut down by the sheer volume of the horde in which they found themselves immersed. The khan's other horsemen cut a swath through the vorgs in front of them, making their way steadily toward the cloud-covered hill where many protectors had gathered.

The slorg screamed, partly in frustration at the mass of vorgs that impeded its progress toward the khan's riders and partly in the pure ecstasy of its killing frenzy. In blind fury it steadily closed the gap that separated it from its quarry. Carol watched in horror, waiting.

In her weakened state, she had been unable to kill the slorg, fire and lightning having no effect. Neither had she been able to strike through the massive shielding that the hundreds of protectors had erected over their hill. She had considerable doubt whether she could pull off what she was about to attempt, but the plan would have to do.

As she circled close to the hill, Carol slid from the mind of one vulture into that of another, this one wearing a black cowl and having two arms instead of wings. As her mind merged with that of the protector who thought of himself as Rogthal, his body stiffened. He struggled against her, just as the priest Angloc had struggled within the body of Jaradin Scot. As the psychic battle raged, she marveled at how similar it was to the mental wrestling match that enabled her to control elementals.

This one was strong, and his consciousness roiled in desperation. Carol closed off one pathway after another until she had the priest's mind locked in a part of his brain where he could do nothing but observe. With a final effort, she seized control of his body. The sensation was mind-bending. She controlled two human bodies: her own, atop a pinnacle several leagues to the east, and the robed form of this madman.

Through his eyes, she looked down the hill to the east. Ty and the khan's horse warriors were now heavily engaged with the large group of special guards kept close to the protectors. Their charge was faltering as wave after wave of the huge vorgs threw themselves at the horsemen, were cut down, and then were replaced by yet another wave of attackers. The slorg was now within a couple of hundred paces of reaching the horsemen's southern flank and only a few hundred paces from where the protectors stood on the hill.

She raised Rogthal's arms and cast, grabbing control of the earth elemental Kevir. A swarm of stones appeared in midair fifteen feet above Rogthal's outstretched hands, the thousands of small spadelike spines whirling about one another and changing shapes rapidly as they darted about. Rogthal's arms whipped forward, directing the swarm outward in the direction he now pointed.

The swarm shot forward above the heads of the elite guard of vorgs surrounding the hill, diving onto the form of the slorg, the stones darting in and out like angry hornets. They stabbed at the rock-hard skin of the monster, rushing in and out of its maw, banging at its eyes in a whirling frenzy. If not for the occasional swat at the swarm from one of its arms, onlookers might have assumed that the beast failed to notice the attack.

As the slorg closed to within a score of paces to the closest of the horsemen, Carol cast once more from Rogthal, this time sending a fireball that erupted in a great geyser of flame as it impacted the slorg. Such was the intensity of the spouting heat that the slorg stopped for an instant.

Carol leapt from the body of the priest, that part of her mind merging with the alien soul of the distant monster. For a second she thought that she would lose herself in the tremendous bloodlust, but then she found that trace of irritation at something other than its target. She thrust into this, her mind fanning the flame to a blistering rage at the gnats who bothered it, the little beings on the hill who had distracted it from what it craved by daring to launch these puny attacks. The rage grew, feeding a different bloodlust stronger than the old.

The slorg turned toward the hill, screamed that terrible scream, and lurched toward its new targets.

With the little strength she could still muster, Carol released herself from the mind of the summoned one, allowing her full consciousness to be sucked back into her own body atop the high pinnacle. The ledge spun beneath her, and she stumbled so that only the grip of Kimber's strong arms kept her from pitching forward off the precipice.

Her head hurt horribly, and she could feel her shields giving way. Shaking her head to clear it, Carol tried to regain focus. She could not falter. Not yet. With supreme effort, she once more strengthened the magical blocks that she held in place. She only hoped that she could stay conscious long enough. From the look on Kim's face, her sister shared similar thoughts.

Carol breathed in deeply of the cool mountain air, letting it fill her lungs and bubble into her bloodstream before slowly exhaling. Once again she straightened her back to stand tall.

—⁊⁊—

Far below, where the narrow ravine gave way to the broad expanse inside the beatific valley of Areana's Vale, High Lord Rafel stood in front of hundreds of soldiers, his closely held reserve. They represented the finest of his soldiers, men who, up until this point, he had held out of the battle, men who clamored to get into the fight to avenge their brothers-in-arms who were dying atop the walls of the westernmost fort. As Rafel saw Carol slump to a knee, then right herself to stand erect once more, a swell of emotion filled his chest and misted his eyes.

But where was Kim? Surely she should also be within his field of view. Rafel pushed aside his anxieties and focused on what he could control.

He turned to face his troops, raised his sword high, and then brought it down in the direction of the forts, a flagman beside him echoing his movements. Then, as a dozen drummers beat out the march, Rafel's reserve strode forward as one.

—⁊⁊—

Gaar walked alongside High Lord Rafel, the drums thundering in his ears. It wasn't bad, as music went, although the only music he needed now was the timpani of battle. For a full night and day, he had been kept out of the battle while he waited and twiddled his thumbs. Might as well have had his thumb up his ass as far as he was concerned.

It all made perfect sense to him, the elite reserve being a strategy he and Rafel had used for many years. Let your enemy come against you until he felt like he was having success and then hit him with a fresh reserve made up of your very best. Shock. Nothing better in battle. Still, being kept out of the fight while your men died before you was the most frustrating thing the old warrior knew.

But now that was about to change. Rafel was finally going to let him get into the fight. He wanted to run ahead down through the sequence of forts and gates until the vorgs surrounded him, offering themselves up to his sword. He whirled his weapon up and around his head, swinging it in massive arcs on each side of his body, letting the wind sing off the blade, warming his arms to the coming battle.

Rafel led the way, with Gaar immediately behind him, followed by a couple of men with signal flags, the drummers, and then the archers, two hundred strong. Gaar spotted John, the one his men had started calling the minstrel for the way his bow sounded when he worked it hard, walking beside the rows of archers, his prominent black eyes visible even from a distance. Behind the bowmen marched the best soldiers in Rafel's army. Gaar recognized them, good souls all.

Behind them appeared the thirty horsemen who accompanied the khan's son, Larok, their bearded faces visible above the others since they were the only ones on mounts.

As they passed down through the gates and drawbridges of the canyon forts, the sound of the drums warmed his blood. These boys weren't bad. The canyon picked up the beat and amplified it so that it boomed back and forth like the sound of a thousand drummers. The synchronized marching of Rafel's armored soldiers crashed in rhythm with the hard central beat, rising to a crescendo as they made their way nearer to the edge of battle. Gaar could barely restrain his feet from dancing. Rafel's demons were coming to dinner.

Up ahead, soldiers parted to let them pass, Hanibal having given the word to clear the way for the counterattack. The noise of battle rose up to meet them as they approached the front lines. The main wall of the lowest fortress had fallen to the enemy, which now controlled more than half of the fort. The wounded and dying were everywhere, being carried to the rear on makeshift stretchers, dripping blood onto the main avenue so that it puddled in the gutters.

At a signal from Rafel a horn sounded, and the archers ran forward, taking up positions along the rear walls of the fort on both sides so that they were looking downward into the inner courtyard to the west. Large stacks of arrows lay in bundles, prepositioned along the walls. Another signal, and the drumming stopped, as did the forward march of Rafel's men.

Once again a horn sounded, this time with the forlorn call of retreat. All along the forward sections of the fort, Hanibal's men turned and fled, abandoning the walls in their race back along the streets. The vorgs screamed in triumph, pouring over the walls and through the gates after the fleeing troops.

As the running men reached the courtyard in front of Rafel, they turned off into a winding side alley that ran along the base of the north wall. Once more the high lord signaled, and the flag-bearers atop the rear walls spun their flags in a circle, bringing them down in unison. The drums thundered through the canyon as Rafel's reserve charged forward.

Gaar roared in delight as he ran, his old legs still conditioned well enough that he could keep up with the lads. The warrior was the first to meet the stunned vorgs that rounded the turn expecting to see soldiers in panicked flight but instead finding themselves facing a rush of fresh troops eager for battle. His sword whirled so fast that its arc blurred, cleaving the snarling vorg in the lead so that the upper half of the man-beast's head flew into the face of the fellows behind him while his legs continued to run forward for three full strides before realizing they were dead.

Immediately the courtyard filled from both directions. Another signal, and two hundred archers unleashed their bolts into the mass of vorgs occupying the western two-thirds of the open space. A second volley followed the first. Then a third was directed out and upward. The storm of bolts arced beyond the far walls to fall into the sea of vorgs jammed into the canyon beyond.

Rafel's soldiers cut their way forward at a run, with Gaar in the lead, taking back the courtyard and then thrusting forward into the street leading back toward the western wall. Another horn sounded, followed almost immediately by a low rumble high up on the cliffs a few hundred paces to the west of the lower fort. The soldiers on those walls unleashed the rockslides onto the horde in the gorge below.

A grun lumbered toward Rafel, sweeping its great spiked club down onto the spot where he had been a moment before, the impact shaking the ground. A buzzing sounded, and arrows began sprouting from the thing's head and neck as it tried to zero in on the warlord. Suddenly it lost its balance, tipping violently as a soldier hacked off its left foot just above the ankle. The crash of the monster's fall sent puffs of dust high into the air, clouds that glinted in the slanting rays of the late afternoon sun, framing the form of the soldier that had leapt atop its back, his sword rising and falling, sending crimson gore spurting in stinking streams.

The vorgs attacking the fort staggered back before the assault. Rafel's men drove into them in disciplined ranks that shoved forward and out like a wedge splitting a log, the lead elements pushing wide so that the forces behind could surge through, continuing the split-ting action. Only Gaar and Rafel refused to peel off to the sides. They pressed forward, always at the tip of the spear.

The leading third of the vorgs had been cut off from their trailing support by the powerful rockslide that crashed down on the forces to their rear. With nothing to push them forward and facing slaughter to their front, they broke and ran. Once again Rafel signaled, and his men poured after the retreating vorgs at a double-quick march, not breaking the formation that only distorted slightly where it was forced to cross the rubble from the slide.

The vorgs raced directly into the mass of their own horde that filled the lower end of the gorge, fighting to get out of the canyon, throwing the follow-on forces into disarray so that the entire lower end of the canyon seemed to boil and bulge. Amidst that cauldron, the elite soldiers of High Lord Rafel's reserve dealt out destruction, holding their ground at the mouth of the ravine.

—ᴍ—

Ty marveled at the change that came across the battle that raged below the protectors' hill. The storm of fire and lightning that heated the magical shielding above the khan's forces instantly stopped as the priesthood tried to stop the slorg, which had abruptly turned its rage toward them. Ty wasn't quite sure why the beast had shifted targets, but the development didn't break his heart.

The slorg's progress slowed as a great storm of lightning, fire, ice, and other pyrotechnics blasted into it. The elite forces that formed the priesthood's inner guard charged, not at the khan's men, but at the slorg.

Ty wheeled his horse away from the hill and raced back to the east, the horsemen matching his movements as if they were an extra appendage. To the north, the army of the protectors had reformed and now pressed forward toward his left flank, cutting off any path back out into the open along that route. A half league to the east lay the entrance to the ravine leading upward to Rafel's fortifications and then Areana's Vale.

Between himself and the canyon, the great army of the vorgs churned in disarray. Some of the forces turned to meet the charge of the khan's men. Others struggled among themselves near the entrance, and although Ty could not be certain, it appeared that Rafel was succeeding in pushing the vorgs out of the ravine with his planned counterattack.

Ty was not to be slowed by waiting for the others, no matter how fast they came. He tore at the trailing edge of the vorgs, cutting them down on the run, adding speed to the stubby legs of those who found no great will to stop and face Ty and the running mass of horsemen a short distance behind him.

The noise of the battlefield was deafening. All about him the clash of armor, the screams of the wounded and dying, the howls of battle fury, and the incessant booming of thunder shook the ground under his horse's hooves. The terrific din drowned out Ty's battle cry. If the land of the dead had a sound, then this must be it. Certainly the numbers that were being sent into that realm with each passing second must have thrown the gateway open wide, so perhaps some of the noise was coming through from the beyond.

The horsemen, though diminished in numbers, added a new disarray to the masses that lay between Ty and his objective, cutting their way forward through a spray of red mist that dripped from riders and their horses as if it was raining. High above, the gods painted the sky scarlet.

As the riders neared the gorge, the sound of drums beat through the other noises. Up ahead Ty could see the leading edge of the line of Rafel's men holding the passage open for him. In front of them, at the center of the line, the soldiers had created a bulge piled high with dead bodies. Without hesitation, Ty cut his way toward that spot, and behind him the horsemen of the khan followed.

Suddenly a wave of arrows arced outward from behind Rafel's line of soldiers, cutting into the vorgs between them and Ty, opening a short gap. The high lord's line parted, and thirty horsemen charged forth. A grin split Ty's face as he watched the khan's son, Larok, lead his platoon forward to link up with his people. When Ty reached him,

Larok whirled around to take the lead, guiding them to the place where Rafel wanted them to ride through his lines. Ty followed Larok through a broad gap that opened to allow them passage as wave after wave of arrows passed outward over their heads.

Ty glanced back over his shoulder as he led the horsemen up the canyon across the bodies of vorgs and men that had died there earlier this day. Rafel's lines closed once more as the last of the horsemen passed through. How many of the riders remained? From the look of it, Ty guessed that not more than a thousand remained alive, many of them slumping in the saddle. So few, less than a third of the host the khan had led into battle just hours before.

Then Ty turned back toward the east, following Larok's lead up the canyon toward Rafel's three forts and the vale that lay beyond.

21

Jorthain limped along through the postmidnight darkness, a faint light illuminating the trail to his tent. Twice he stumbled and would have fallen had not Boban reached out to steady him. Jorthain glanced over at the wizened priest who served as his aide. The small, piggish eyes gleamed in a face framed by long gray hair that hung nearly to the man's belt. His mouth, like a slash in a side of beef, appeared to have no lips. In fact, Jorthain could not think of one redeeming quality in the withered Boban.

He was a coward, completely untrustworthy, and as stupid as one of the vorgs. Perhaps that combination was what attracted Jorthain to the man. Here was a servant of ultimate loyalty, too imbecilic to think of a plan to undermine his master's authority, too cowardly to try such a plan if he thought of it, and too unpopular to get any support from others should he overcome the first two insurmountable deficiencies. Yes, he was the perfect aide.

As Jorthain staggered into his tent, sinking into the deep pile of throw pillows in exhaustion, he waved Boban away.

"No one is to disturb me until dawn!" he yelled after the man. "Have the Conclave of the Nine assembled in front of my tent by then." Jorthain stretched his thin arms over his head, yawning deeply. He was tired to the point that he was having difficulty finding his way into sleep. Unbelievable. A day that had started so well had gone badly wrong.

He had known that the witch was powerful, but never had he imagined that she could fend off more than two hundred priests for such a long time. Yes, they had felt periodic weaknesses in her defenses, but even those may have been traps intended to plant seeds of overconfidence. The high priest had also been taken aback by the twin counterattacks, clearly well planned and coordinated, which had driven his forces from the canyon and had disrupted his army to the point that it would take at least two full days to get reorganized for the final assault.

Neither had Jorthain anticipated the arrival of the high-country horsemen. In all recorded history, he had never heard of them asking for help or giving aid to others, content to keep to themselves in their mountain stronghold, maintaining a strong neutrality that kept them safe. And yet they had dared to join forces with these people in defiance of his priesthood. So be it. On the morrow, he would send a few thousand of his soldiers along the horsemen's back trail so that the vorgs might introduce themselves to their wives and children.

Had that been the sum total of the unexpected series of his misfortunes, he would have been frustrated and angry, certainly. However, cap that off with the summoning of the slorg, and it was the perfect end to a dreadful day. Jorthain wished that he could do a casting of his own, one that would recall from the dead that idiot of idiots who had gotten the brilliant idea to sacrifice himself for the glory of the destruction that the slorg would dole out to the horsemen.

Rigo always had a misguided sense of loyalty to the dark gods. This time the fool had offered himself up as a temple of destruction for their enemies, all on his own, without consultation with his high priest or his fellows. Rigo had given no thought to the notion that once the slorg was finished killing all its initial targets, it would turn on everyone nearby until its bloodlust was sated. Then and only then could the doleful beast be sent back to its realm.

The witch. Jorthain mulled over what she had apparently done, rejected the idea as implausible, reconsidered, and then rejected it once again. Whatever the cause, the slorg had diverted from its original target, killing forty-seven priests and many hundreds of his inner guard before it was satisfied to the point that it could be gated out. Diverting a slorg was supposed to be impossible. The witch could not have done that. No, it must have been that idiot Rigo failing to clearly visualize his target as the slorg consumed him.

The wistful image of Rigo chained to a table as Jorthain extracted his eyes with hot tongs finally allowed the high priest to drift off into a deep sleep.

22

Glacier Mountains, Southeast of Endar Pass
YOR 415, Mid-Spring

Kragan raced up the steep hillside, powerful legs propelling his seven-foot-tall primordial form as his arms flung aside any of his soldiers who were unable to scramble out of his way. He could have called upon Ohk to conjure an invisible platform on which he could stand, but he felt a burning need to watch from the ridgetop what was unfolding.

For more than a week, his scouts had hunted for the Endarian mist warriors who had fled the battlefield after Kragan had killed their time-shaper. Their flight had been a wise move, if not a particularly brave one. During that time, Kragan had kept his army marching toward Endar. The progression was not rapid given his army's foraging requirements. It was impossible to move a force of more than one hundred thousand swiftly, especially through lands without towns to raid or farms to scavenge.

Reaching the crest, Kragan stared out over the evolving battle in the valley beyond, excited by the sight that confronted him. Once again the time-mists flowed down along the steep slopes on the north side of the canyon and into the leading edge of his forces.

So, Kaleal's voice sounded in Kragan's mind, *the Endarian retreat was a ruse to pull us into an ambush.*

"Just as I said they would," said Kragan, causing nearby soldiers to glance around to see who he was talking to. "The mist warriors have another time-shaper within their ranks."

This one uses different patterns than the last.

A sneer curled Kragan's lips. "It matters not. I have a surprise in store for them."

—✲—

Galad shoved aside his frustration at not being the commander who was leading his time-mist warriors into battle and focused all his attention on channeling the mists within which they would fight. As he had rehearsed with Commander Tempas and her subordinate leaders, he wove the mists that flowed out and cut across the ranks of Kragan's lead elements. The morning was bright and crystal clear, with a brisk breeze that swept down from the glaciers that lay to his west. From this vantage point overlooking the field of battle, he observed the shrouds obscure all whom they enveloped. As had become standard procedure, he used the mists to separate chunks of Kragan's soldiers, allowing the Endarian warriors to exercise their battle skills.

In the meantime, Galad studied the seemingly endless columns of marching vorgs, some of whom surged wide to either side of the valley, attempting to encircle those who fought within the mists. That tactic was not going to work.

Galad channeled new mists, sending the pomaly fog out in front of the enemies that charged around the Endarian left and right flanks. He balanced the slowing with a fresh river of rychly mists that his warriors could utilize. The vorgs who charged around the left flank jammed up as the lead ranks struggled into the pomaly fogbank that blocked their path. Galad nodded in satisfaction as he watched the same thing happen to the enemies trying to flank the Endarians on the other side.

He did not have time to savor the moment. To avoid succumbing to the same tactic that Kragan had employed to kill Laikas, it was time to move to his second overlook.

Galad stepped from normal time into the first layer of rychly mist, feeling the familiar drag from behind until he stepped all the way into the accelerated zone. In the canyon far below, he saw new mists form. No longer able to see the bulk of Kragan's army, he did observe Endarians and some vorgs passing through the winding channel. But Galad did not stop to study their movements, continuing instead into faster and faster mists until he found the one that would take him to his desired destination while little time passed in the normal world.

He stepped onto the overlook and was prepared to make the transitions that would place him back in standard time when he saw something that froze him in place. In the bottom of the canyon, several hundred mist warriors prepared an ambush for the vorg archers who slowly emerged from the mist. But to Galad's horror, he saw a broad swath of the enemy archers thrust their bows, arms, and heads through the mist wall, able to release their arrows long before the rest of their bodies pulled free of the slower zone.

The vorgs had adopted one of the mist warrior tactics to devastating effect. Even though the Endarians countered with their own volley of arrows, their warriors dropped by the score.

Worse, four of the leather- and chain mail–clad vorgs dropped their bows to launch fireballs and summon lightning. The realization that Kragan's wielders had disguised themselves so that the Endarians could not immediately target them stunned Galad.

He channeled two new mists, sending these coursing down the mountainside toward the distant battle. If he had been closer to the front lines, his action would have allowed hundreds of his people to escape the conflagration. But to Galad's utter despair, he was too far away to observe the subtle swirling within the mists that would tell him what moved within the fogs. Before the first tendrils of these new mists could separate the Endarians from enemies, hundreds more vorgs emerged to launch the next wave of arrows at the surviving mist warriors.

"No!" Galad's cry resounded throughout the open passage that wound its way through the fog, causing some vorgs to turn toward the ledge upon which he stood. But as one of Kragan's wielders raised his hand to cast a spell, Galad thrust himself into a different mist.

When he arrived at the designated rally point, his dread found its source as the full extent of the Endarian defeat became clear. The survivors numbered less than half of the fifteen hundred who had followed him from Endar. Of those, more than a hundred had suffered serious wounds.

He moved among the wounded with Commander Tempas at his side, pausing to give an encouraging word or a reassuring touch, fighting to keep the sickness in his soul from showing itself. Galad watched as the brigade's two remaining life-shifters worked to separate those who must be allowed to die so that they could treat a greater number of the less severely injured.

When he left the wounded, Galad felt like hundreds of Endarian eyes followed him. He could feel those stares like a lead vest trying to drag him to his knees. Despite his mist-weaving having let them down, these warriors now looked to him to make matters right. As he came to a stop before them, he realized he had no idea how to do that.

"Tempas," he said, fighting to keep his voice steady, "this is my fault. I should have known that I could not replace Laikas."

She placed a hand on his arm. "My friend, Laikas could not have prevented what happened on this day."

Galad turned to meet Tempas's gaze. "You're wrong about that. I should have wielded the mists better."

"What we were missing during today's attack was not your ability to wield the time-mists. We missed your unique ability to sense what moves beyond those misty walls. We have grown used to you leading us in battle. Without you at our head, we were blind."

A sour taste filled Galad's mouth. "I cannot simultaneously command mist warriors in battle and channel the mists within which they must fight."

"How do you know that if you've never tried?"

The question left Galad silent for a moment.

"My first attempt to do so should not come in battle."

"You must resume your command if any of us hope to see Endar again."

Galad paced slowly back and forth, rubbing his chin as he considered this. Coming to a decision, he stopped, his eyes on Tempas's battle-scarred face.

"Very well. Tonight we will rest and let the life-shifters do their work. Tomorrow we will begin fighting our way back to Endar."

"Good," said Tempas. "I will inform our warriors."

As Galad watched his second-in-command turn and walk away, a painful lump formed in his throat. Never before had he gone home in defeat. This time he would return to his queen with less than half of the elite mist warriors that he had led out of Endar Pass. And he would be bearing with him the body of Laikas, the fairest soul he had ever known.

PART IV

In my dreams, I see the woman who bears the elemental mark on her shoulder. She stands atop a lonely pinnacle wrapped in cascading webs of power. A cloak drapes her slender shoulders, its color shifting from white to red as she moves. I fear that she wears the fate of this world.

—From the *Scroll of Landrel*

23

Val'Dep
YOR 415, Mid-Spring

As much as Alan hated being left behind, he disliked his new taskmaster even more. The leader of the khan's rearguard was an older, peg-legged soldier named Kron, whose wiry ugliness was surpassed only by his bitter disposition. From all accounts, the man had been a legendary horseman and warrior in his day and the khan's guard. All those careers had come to a sudden halt when his horse fell during battle, mangling his leg so badly that it had required amputation. Since that day, the khan had assigned Kron the task of training the warriors in their weapon skills. He had also placed Kron in charge of the defense of Val'Dep whenever the khan was gone.

Now Val'Dep stood defenseless. The khan had left only one company of warriors behind, along with Alan's platoon of thirty men, one hundred and fifty fighting men in total. In addition, they had perhaps four hundred older men and boys strong enough to bear weapons. The rest were women, small children, the elderly, and the infirm, several thousand in all. Only the incredible natural barriers of the mountain fortress city made a defense thinkable under such circumstances.

The clean central street of the eastern half of Val'Dep wound its way upward toward the high palace in front of Alan. The morning sunshine did little to lift his mood as he strode upward. High above, the cooing of the doves caused him to lift his gaze to the towers above the south wall of the city. Barely visible in the distance beyond the gently fluttering banners, black thunderheads climbed high into the otherwise blue sky.

A deeply worried Alan shook his head and increased his pace, barely noticing Bill's lanky form behind him. There was little doubt that beneath those shadow skies, men fought and died in a battle that should have been his. And what was he doing in the meantime? Preparing defenses against a possible counterattack? No. Not even that solace was granted him. Kron had seized all the tasks associated with getting the men and lads ready for battle and had named Alan his deputy. Deputy indeed. Handmaiden was a more fitting title considering his assignment.

Passing beneath the ornate horse fresco carvings of the gateway to the upper palace, Alan returned the salutes of the two guardsmen and walked into the palace courtyard. Just inside, he stopped, Bill coming to a halt beside him.

"Well, I'm ready if you are," the young ranger said, grinning at him. It was funny that Alan thought of Bill as young since he was a year older than Alan. But the events of the last few months had made the lord feel older.

"Great gods, how am I ever going to get a girl with you this close all the time?" Alan asked him.

Bill just put forth a grin and shrugged. "Just imagine I'm not here."

"Oh, yeah," Alan had replied. "That's gonna happen."

Now the two gathered their strength for the meeting they dreaded more than facing a vorg army. Not more than twenty feet away from where they now stood, they would pass into a meeting hall where a most fearsome audience awaited.

The Council of Matrons of Val'Dep.

With slumped shoulders, Alan marched forward once again.

The women of the council raised their heads as he entered, his entrance apparently having disrupted a huddle of some importance.

The Council of Matrons had been an important fixture of the society for many hundreds of years and was made up of older citizens widely regarded as the top experts in the city in all womanly roles and responsibilities. These responsibilities encompassed a wide gauntlet of tasks, including baking, cooking, tailoring, mending of armor, gardening and farming, general cleaning, washing of clothing, nursing and doctoring, the gathering of food and water from the fields and wells . . . and on and on the list went. Even butchering was considered a woman's task since it fit in with the gathering and preparation of meals.

The matrons were not elected; it simply became apparent to others over time which one of the women was in charge of an area. While there had been famous squabbles in years past where two or more women had vied for a single position, the system worked more smoothly than most political structures. The process certainly produced a group of assertive women, a fact that had become brilliantly clear to Alan on the previous day when Kron had assigned him the glorious task of organizing the ladies in support of the main defensive effort.

His initial meeting had not gone well, to put it mildly, perhaps due primarily to his bad attitude. He was certain that his father had not assigned such demeaning duty to the khan's son. This was nothing short of an outrage, although one he had been given no choice but to accept. As it was, his opening statement was a no-nonsense demand that the matrons listen so that he could assign them tasks appropriate to their stations. What followed closely resembled what Alan imagined throwing open the gates of the deep to be like.

He would not have believed it possible to have that many fingers waggling in his face simultaneously. How could that many large older women move so fast? How could so many crowd into such a tight space?

How could they possibly yell that loudly and continue for such a long time without tiring?

Thank the gods he had managed to quiet down the group enough that he could beg their pardon for his poor choice of manner and words. Only by promising to spend the evening in the tutelage of the chief matron, who would endeavor to make him understand the honored role of each member of the council before he next came before them, was he allowed to escape with a small fraction of his hearing intact.

As he had been instructed by Loraine, the chief matron, the evening before, the words of the formal greeting tumbled from his mouth as he and Bill inclined their heads in a deep bow.

"Good women of the council, I beseech you to grant me audience that we may discuss matters of great urgency."

The three dozen women simultaneously straightened their backs and dipped into a deep curtsy in response, a sight so startling that Alan had to struggle to keep a straight face.

Loraine was the first to resume a normal posture, her movement mirrored by the other matrons. "You are most welcome indeed, Lord Rafelson."

Alan did not attempt to correct her as to the matter of his name, instead choosing to recover from the ridiculous bow.

For more than two hours, the meeting ground along with an assortment of procedural matters that seemed to Alan to be designed to waste everyone's time when there was very little of that commodity to waste. Finally Loraine clapped her hands twice and rose to speak.

"Matrons of Val'Dep, this brings us to the matter at hand. I believe that our young guest has come to understand that what he may very well regard as unnecessary process and procedure is all that stands between the tasks that he desires our cooperation with and complete chaos.

"We have not spent twenty-five generations keeping the affairs of Val'Dep running like clockwork without discovering that certain preliminary steps are necessary in all matters if we are to conduct business efficiently.

"In my long session with the young man last night, I must admit that I was at first skeptical that he would be fit for the task of guiding us in our preparations for war. I thought it highly likely that he was merely another noble hothead, all bellow and bluster, only good for swinging that ax of his and little else. But surprisingly, he impressed me."

Loraine's gaze swept her audience, lingering on Alan for a moment.

"Oh now, don't get me wrong. Lord Rafelson is most definitely hotheaded, but the heat is the heat of passion. What impressed me is that no matter how distasteful he found his task of being liaison to the matrons of Val'Dep instead of to the warriors of Val'Dep, no matter how much he didn't want to spend ten hours of the evening and night listening to an old battle-ax like myself, he did so. And not only did he sit there; he paid attention, listened, and learned. And he accepted his role in all this.

"I sense within this young lord a drive, nay, a work ethos that compels him to do whatever he must to the best of his abilities. Unless I miss my guess, which I seldom do . . ."—a whisper of laughter bubbled around the edges of the room—". . . those abilities are considerable. While he still knows very little of the total that makes up our way of things, Lord Rafelson has a feel for war beyond his age.

"Therefore I want you to pay close attention to what he says. It will be the task of each of us to scour his words for guidance and then to use our own innovative ways to figure out how best we can aid the effort."

With a wave of her hand, she signaled that the meeting was handed over to Alan.

Alan rose somewhat stiffly to his feet. Oddly, a deep sense of pride swelled his chest. To think that here, in this room full of mature women, he had finally shown the leadership and composure his father had always longed to see Alan exhibit. A flood of new worries about giving false hope to these women and the inherent inadequacies of the plan he was to propose coursed through his mind. But he cleared his throat and continued.

"Thank you, Chief Matron Loraine, and indeed to all of you, the matrons of Val'Dep. As the chief matron has said, we are all but out of time. We can't afford to make any other assumption."

The matrons seated in groups around tables within the room nodded in agreement.

Alan stretched out his hand, pointing toward the south wall of the meeting hall.

"Beyond that wall, outside of this city, just a day's ride to our south, your warriors and mine are engaged in a terrible battle. The odds are that they cannot win it."

Several gasps around the room showed the shock his statement caused.

"I have seen up close the army our peoples face, and it is monstrous. To have any chance of winning, we have to maximize every advantage we have. Our warriors are trained, fearless, and disciplined. We have great natural defensive positions. The problem is that our enemies vastly outnumber us."

As Alan paused, the silence in the room gathered until it took on an oppressive weight. He left the head table to stride among the gathering of stout citizens.

"As she said, your chief talked to me last night, and I listened to her counsel. What I learned is that in Val'Dep, more than in any society I have heard of, the women are an organized force that does most of the work, freeing the men to ride about practicing whirling their axes and looking fine."

Laughter erupted in the room, accompanied by the nodding of heads. Having captured their full attention, Alan continued.

"And that is a good thing. You have given your men a chance to be the best at what they do. You have done that by being the best at all the other tasks that make your society function. In a short period of time, a couple of days at most, I expect that a significant portion of that malevolent army will march into your valley and launch themselves against these ramparts, expecting to find the walls manned by a skeletal force of warriors, the old, and the very young.

"Their intent will be to batter their way through those meager forces and then rape, loot, and pillage among the women and children who remain, to take the ones they want as slaves, killing everyone else, burning and destroying everything in their path. We are going to ensure that they are in for a terrible surprise."

As Alan talked, the matrons leaned forward, drinking in his words, a look of cold determination growing in their faces. He talked of how the battle would go, how the ravine that blocked access to the outer wall was a mighty barrier but not unbreachable. The vorgs would come at it with ramps and ladders. Some would make it to the top of the wall, where they would attempt to gain control of the gargantuan winches that operated the khan's ramps.

The vorgs would focus on these, trying to get them lowered so that the mass could surge upward in such numbers that those at the top would be overwhelmed. Once over the outer wall, the battle would be done, since there would not be enough troops left to man the khan's layered defenses.

Alan paced the room as he talked, moving among the tables, although his eyes had taken on a distant look as if he were even now looking out across the battlefield. Suddenly he stopped once more at the head table, looking directly into the chief matron's steel-blue eyes.

"I know what we need to do to give ourselves a chance of victory. But you are the ones who know precisely what all the women under your direction can do, and I will need you to come up with inventive ways to make that work for us to ensure our survival."

Once more Alan paused, sweeping the room with his gaze.

"There is one more thing I should mention, which may get me in trouble with you once again. I believe that no matter how well the few soldiers, old men, and young lads fight, it will not be enough to save this city. I therefore have no intention of limiting your roles to only those tasks that Commander Kron has delegated to us. We will plan on fighting this battle as if there were no one out there to fight for us." He paused. "If you are willing to do so."

A new thought struck Alan as he looked out over the sea of surprised and enthusiastic faces. Apparently Carol's philosophy of equality of the sexes had infected him.

A cheer erupted in the room, and once again, Alan found himself on the verge of being smothered by large women.

Having moved to a safe place in the far corner, Bill chuckled long and hard.

—⁙—

A lull settled over the battlefield for a day after Rafel's counterattack had reestablished control of the canyon and the khan's men had fought their way into the valley. Kim begged Carol to rest, just for a little while, and in brief stretches she managed to do so. Using the eyes of the vultures, she could see the disarray of the enemy forces, but a massive effort was underway to reorganize the horde for another attack. The protectors probed at her defenses, but Carol's early warning network of minor elementals alerted her to each attempt.

But now she saw what she had dreaded. More than two thousand vorgs and their allies had split off from the main body of the army to march north in the direction of Val'Dep. Moreover, three of the most powerful protectors accompanied them.

Alan was out there. She could feel her brother's desperate need growing. Try as she might, she could not imagine how the fortress of Val'Dep could stand against the numbers that marched toward it, not with the remainder of the khan's warriors trapped within Areana's Vale.

It was a choice that the khan had knowingly made, but his gamble had failed. She willed the vulture north, circling above the division of vorgs as they jogged along in formation.

Come the morrow, she must be ready with enough reserves to provide cover to Val'Dep. At least Alan could die a warrior's death without being blasted off the ramparts by sorcery.

A cool breeze ruffled her red-stained white shirt as she rose to face northeast. As Kim stood at her side, tears made their way down Carol's cheeks.

—⚭—

Despite his earlier misgivings, Alan found himself awed by how quickly the matrons organized the women of Val'Dep and got them moving. Loraine had placed the youngest, oldest, and weakest of the women in charge of caring for the small children. They had moved this vulnerable population to locations deep within the northeastern part of the split city. This left three thousand women available who were fit to work or fight.

Alan had taken to calling her "Chief." Even though this had initially caused some raised eyebrows, she seemed to enjoy the title, so it stuck. Both she and the matrons under her command proved highly adept at completing a wide variety of tasks quickly. Based upon Alan's general guidance, they had determined how the women could best support his strategy.

He had laid out the battle in phases, the first of which would be the initial struggle for the wall. During this phase, the women were to comply with Commander Kron's intent and limit themselves to a support role, delivering food and supplies to the wall and caring for the wounded.

The second phase of battle would be when the defenses atop the wall began to crumble. At that point, all women capable of fighting would move into direct combat roles while the others continued to provide support.

The third phase would occur if the outer wall fell. Alan referred to this as the "prepare to die" phase. They did not bother to plan for it.

Loraine organized slightly more than half the women into support groups that would continue to have the same role during both phases of the battle. Sewing circles became fletching circles, and bakers made the flat bread that would serve as meals for the coming days. Groups of women drew water and routed it down wooden troughs to fill tanks behind the outer wall. Prepositioned firewood and oil augmented the bundles of arrows, bandages, and other combat-support materials.

The more challenging task was to convert the remaining women into a capable combat force. One solution was archery. Alan made clear that he did not care in the least about their accuracy.

"If we get to the point that you're having a hard time being accurate enough to hit one of the bastards coming at us, then we've won," he said.

What he wanted was a high volume of fire that would reach at least a hundred feet. If a woman could not pull a bowstring that would launch an arrow that far, then she was not a candidate for the position. This turned out not to be a problem since these women had spent their lives doing heavy manual labor of every conceivable type. An unexpected advantage was that many of the women thus had exceptional manual dexterity. Using quick hands and fingers, they could launch a stream of arrows swiftly since they only had to aim in a general given direction.

The chief selected close to eleven hundred women as archers, immediately setting them to work making more stacks of arrows to augment the stockpiles already available and moving them into cache positions near the outer wall. She also set up a flag signaling system for simple aiming and firing commands, such as high, low, right, middle, and left.

Moira, matron of the harvest, resolved the problem of how to form a more direct fighting force from a group of women untrained in combat. While none of the women was skilled in the use of a sword, ax, or battle hammer, several hundred women had years of experience in the fields using a farming implement called a ukeel, which looked like a cross between a scythe and a spear. The ukeel had a pace-long staff that ended in a sharp double-edged blade and a triangular spadelike point. The women used it to harvest both wheat and hay crops, with sweeping strokes that rose high on one side, slashing down and across the crop, followed by reversing the stroke.

In planting season, the sharp point of the ukeel formed the perfect implement. Its user thrust forward and down into the soil, giving the tool a quick turn to loosen the dirt once it was embedded in the ground. Once he had seen its use demonstrated, Alan could see no reason why the same motions would not work for harvesting and planting vorgs.

Once the women had accepted the idea of using implements they were already comfortable using instead of trying to teach them to use the traditional instruments of war, a cascade of possibilities presented themselves. The chief soon had companies of meat carvers armed with cleavers and butcher knives and even a group of fishwives armed with spears and nets.

Armor turned out not to be a problem, the quantity of chain-mail vests in storage being ample for a force twice as large. Alan found some difficulty in suppressing a grin at the sight of some of the bustier women trying to find a set that fit in a way that was not too constricting. To get them used to the feel, the chief matron ordered that all the women, including those in support roles, wear the chain-mail vests under their work clothes at all times.

—⚏—

Standing atop a section of the wall where he could watch the women work in the late afternoon sun, Alan felt more than heard Bill step up beside him.

"That is a strange-looking lot you have assembled."

Alan nodded, his gaze sweeping across the thousands of women covering the parade grounds around the central dais holding the ivory throne of the khan. "They will do their best. No man could ask any more of people under his command."

A single note of a horn sounded, and Alan turned to see a lone rider coming hard. Only one of the two huge ramps remained lowered into place, and onto this the rider raced, sliding to a halt along the broad rampart at the top, dismounting on the fly. Alan ran forward as Kron hobbled over to meet the rider.

The messenger motioned to the southwest with his outstretched arm. "They are coming."

"How many and how far out?" asked Kron.

"Over two thousand," said the statuesque warrior. "At the rate they're moving, they will reach our walls before dawn."

"And the khan?"

"No sign of any of our people. It would seem that they failed." The warrior slumped with the utterance.

Kron straightened, his scarred face taking on a mask even grimmer than his normal appearance. "So it would seem. Get your horse taken care of and then join your men at their station."

Without a word, the bearded rider leapt onto his mount and galloped down the sod ramp that led downward from the back side of the fortress wall. Ignoring Alan, Kron spun in a hopping motion, balanced on his peg leg.

"Raise and secure the ramp!"

His yell echoed across the canyon, followed by the squeal and rattle of chains as the massive winch swung the ramp slowly up and away from the far side of the gorge.

24

Glacier Mountains, Southeast of Endar
YOR 415, Mid-Spring

In the last disastrous battle, Galad had isolated himself in the role of time-shaper and had thus failed to recognize that Kragan's twin attempts to encircle the Endarians had merely been feints. Kragan had actually sent twin divisions of vorgs in two wider pincer movements. While what remained of Galad's brigade had regrouped and reorganized at their rally point, Kragan had closed his vise around them, cutting off the mist warriors' escape route back to Endar Pass.

Knowing that he and his entire brigade were as good as dead, Galad was left to make the choice of how they would die . . . defending or attacking. Having decided to resume his command of what remained of his brigade, he knew which choice he would make.

With his bow strapped across his back, he summoned the mists, sending tendrils out through the forest and up the rugged mountainside to the northwest. If he and his warriors had to die today, they would do so fighting their way toward their homeland.

What he was about to try was unthinkable. As far as he knew, no time-shaper had ever even attempted the feat. But Galad was not only a time-shaper; he was a warrior with the unheard-of ability to sense subtle variations in the mists to guide his brigade's attacks. While it was impossible to see what lay on the far side of those foglike vapors, Galad could sense the disturbances in the boundaries. And those small motions painted a picture of what moved within rychly and pomaly zones. Over the years, he had come to understand that this ability was related to his talent for channeling time-mists.

Yesterday, he had mistakenly secluded himself away from battle as all other time-shapers did in order to maintain their concentration. Never again. With a curt command to his signalperson, Galad ordered his six hundred warriors forward. With sword in hand, he led them into the mists.

As Galad stepped into the swirling curtain of rychly fog, he drew upon it even as it dissipated around him, sending new tendrils spreading out before him, changing the way time flowed as he walked. Controlling the mists as he maneuvered through them was the oddest feeling he had ever experienced. He was actually directing the churning mists that surrounded him with his mind without the meditative hand gesturing that he had been taught. Just as importantly, he was able to simultaneously engulf his mist warriors within the same flow of time through which he moved.

Up ahead in the fog within which he and his mist warriors strode, he saw the hundred-pace-wide passage that this zone had formed end in an off-white pomaly fogbank. As he approached the wall he slowed to a halt, allowing the leading ranks of his brigade to step up even with him. Focusing his senses, Galad studied the patterns that moved within the milky haze. There could be no doubt. Many beings lay beyond that obscurity. He could sense the enemy's ranks moving slowly and at an oblique angle to him.

Galad raised his sword, drawing an arc that extended across his front and then away from the fogbank on his right, a movement that his signalperson emulated. His warriors shifted the formation. The first two ranks of one hundred remained in place, while most of the bowmen moved off to the right to form the arc that Galad had traced. With graceful precision from years of experience under his command, they faced back toward him, their bows at the ready.

Galad inhaled deeply, savoring the tang of pine and the warmth of the morning sun on his back. At his signal, the two ranks of mist warriors in line with him nocked arrows and drew them taut.

Then, instead of stepping through the pomaly curtain, Galad summoned the mists forward.

—◊—

Charna, Kragan's she-vorg commander, heard the cries of alarm and turned to see the fog along her army's left flank suddenly dissipate, revealing a couple of hundred archers. The Endarians released three quick volleys, cutting a swath through the vorgs who turned to meet them.

Her eyes were drawn to the Endarian in the center, who had a slender sword in his hand. He gestured with it, and the mists swirled in to hide those who had launched the sudden attack. Farther down the ridge to the southeast, another bank of fog retreated, revealing an arc of hundreds more warriors, who fired volleys into the same area that the first group had targeted.

With a growl, Charna ordered the attack. Her flag-bearer gave the command that launched a thousand vorgs toward the roiling mists that once again shifted in to hide the attackers just in time to quench the fireball that streaked toward the distant bowmen. Suddenly that charge faltered as four tendrils of fog snaked outward toward the vorgs.

What in the deep was happening here? This new time-mist wielder was using tactics unlike any other Charna had yet faced. And when those murky tentacles rolled over her troops, it was as if the Endarian had driven a spear into the heart of the charge.

Charna looked out over the division of vorgs that had encircled the mist warriors on the northwest, cutting off their retreat toward Endar. The vorgs struggled to respond to the attacks that branched up the heavily wooded mountainside from the southeast. She cast about her, looking for Silap or any of the other three wielders who had accompanied Charna's forces on the pincer maneuver. But the confusion of the forces fighting in the thick woods frustrated her efforts to see the sorcerers.

She turned to her captain of the guard. "Hilbin. With me."

Then Charna hefted her war hammer and raced toward turmoil's heart, trailed by a company of her elite.

—∾—

The vorg archers directly in front of Galad raised their bows in unison just as he channeled a fresh rychly mist that rose to embrace his warriors. At his signal, his brigade moved away from the line of fire, then watched as the storm of arrows emerged from the mists like bean shoots sprouting from the soil. They fell impotently to the ground several paces farther.

Having moved off to one side, the Endarian ranks reformed, bows at the ready. When the leading vorgs who had charged after them slowly clawed their way into the rychly zone, Galad's bowmen loosed fresh volleys, felling vorgs in waves. Despite the destruction raining down on them, the surviving attackers returned fire, felling a score of Endarian warriors before Galad could channel another wall of mist.

Pulse racing, Galad led his warriors directly up the mountain to the north into the thick woods that draped its sides. Although his muscles felt fresh, the effort he was putting into channeling time was rapidly making him groggy. Shunting fatigue aside, he siphoned murky tendrils toward the weak spot his brigade had punched in the vorg lines. His hazy shroud flowed over his soldiers and into another group of surprised vorgs, who now found themselves staring directly into a new arrow storm. Galad sprinted through the trees and ducked left and then right, at the head of six hundred warriors who had exchanged their bows for swords.

Having closed with the enemy within the trees, Galad whirled among them, his flashing sword biting deep. Suddenly a new company of vorgs charged into the fray, led by a large female wielding a war hammer. When their eyes met, she snarled and came straight for him.

Galad ducked under the hammer that whizzed past his ear, the air howling like a wounded animal. He stabbed at her torso, but the blade glanced off her chain mail. Again the she-vorg struck at him, and Galad stepped aside, inflicting a cut across the back of her forearm. As they continued their contest, all around them mist warriors and vorgs clashed. The shrieks of the wounded mingled with the ring of steel on steel.

Lightning arced through the air, striking the ground in the midst of the vorgs and Endarians. The energy knocked Galad and his opponent to the ground. Galad stared up through the trees as they whirled around him. He reached out, grabbed a low branch, and pulled himself back to his feet.

This was the moment, the inflection point where the battle could turn with just one mighty push. Fighting through the vertigo that dulled his thoughts, Galad channeled two rivers of mist, the lighter pomaly fog flowing directly west, where the bulk of the vorgish division had massed. The darker rychly mist formed a narrow passage that wound its way up the ridge to the northeast.

Yelling the command echoed by other nearby mist warriors, he plunged into rychly fog even as the slower zone he was leaving tried to hold him back. Other Endarians emerged, bloody from combat but turning to kill any vorgs who attempted to follow. Up ahead, besides the dozens of vorgs that the mist had captured, the passage was relatively clear.

Galad and his warriors charged, their blades dispatching those who tried to stop them. As he sprinted forward, working to extend the time-mist farther up and over the ridge, the vertigo returned. He realized that he had overtaxed his channel, but he pressed on. Galad didn't realize he had fallen until the ground smacked him face-first. Then he felt powerful hands lift his body.

He caught a brief glimpse of Captain Tempas's worried gaze as she tossed him over her left shoulder. Then the whirling forest winked out.

25

Val'Dep
YOR 415, Mid-Spring

Alan had watched the vorgs pour into the narrow valley since four hours before dawn, their torches a sea of fireflies moving ever closer. Overhead lightning danced in the sky, an obvious display of strength from their wielder priests. Now as the first light in the east hinted at dawn's approach, a mighty thrumming and chanting arose from not more than a half league southwest of the chasm that ran at the base of the fortress wall of Val'Dep. The noise was louder than the rumble of the waterfall that plunged off the southeast canyon wall into the depths of the gorge below.

Despite the thunderheads gathering above, the sky gradually lightened as dawn broke, although it was a dark dawn to be sure. The forward lines of the invaders had formed up a few hundred paces away, two large siege engines with mechanical ramps visible in the foreground. The vorgs in the formation bobbed up and down in their desire to charge, like barrels on a stormy sea.

Kron gave Alan's thirty men the task of defending the far-right end of the wall, an idiotic move since the center section was the most vulnerable. Both of the khan's ramps were mounted there; one swung left and the other right in their raised positions. The vorgs would go for these, and while the khan had left just over a hundred good men to anchor the defense, most of the manning consisted of old men or lads barely into their midteens. To position thirty experienced soldiers on the flank was an infuriating lapse in judgment. But Kron wanted nothing to do with Alan or his people.

As for the women, Alan had decided to leave Kron unaware of his plan to use them in battle when things went badly. All the women wore their normal loose work dresses, but underneath they wore their chain vests and breeches. They had added an extra seam to their dresses so that, on command, they could throw them off to allow extra freedom of movement.

Alan's final audience with the Council of Matrons had concluded with his asking for their acquiescence in this part of the plan. The chief spoke for them all.

"That old fool Kron would rather sacrifice us to the gods of war than consider that women could be used for aught more than bearing children and tending to the men. This is our fight, every bit as much as it is the men's, and our blood and the blood of our children are going to flow just as red should we lose. If it must be spilled, then I say let it be done while slitting vorg gullets. We will fight!"

The other women nodded in stern agreement.

"So be it," said Alan, his finger pointing out an imaginary line behind the wall. "As we planned then, the women will all start out doing the support work. Make sure that you distribute all your archers along the line, not more than fifty feet from the back side of the wall. Let them be part of the bucket brigade passing supplies forward or stoking the fires, whatever will make them inconspicuous in their areas.

"They will be near prepositioned stacks of bows and arrows. At the signal, they will cast off the gowns that hide their armor, grab their bows, and begin firing high over the wall, letting their arrows rain down beyond. The flag signals, or torch signals if it is dark, will guide them in the general directions we want to concentrate their fire. In the absence of that, have them shoot high arcing shots directly forward of their positions.

"The other signal will be a call for the fighting women of Val'Dep to charge to the wall. They will rush forward with ukeel, cleaver, knife, or spear. They fight for the lives of their children and loved ones inside the city. I have seen a she-bear in defense of her cubs. Let us introduce that bear to the vorgs."

A murmur of agreement passed among the matrons.

"They are all yours, Chief," Alan said.

Loraine turned to the others, her eyes ablaze. "Have them ready. Be off with you."

Alan could still see their faces in his mind's eye. These women had no illusions that they were likely to prevail. Their looks all said as much. All they wanted was a chance to strike a blow for their people. He had a feeling they were going to get that opportunity soon enough.

A triple fork of lightning struck downward at the wall, the pitchfork prongs bending away at the last instant, reflecting outward into the mass of vorgs as a simultaneous blast of thunder shook the ground. Another bolt followed the first, and it, too, was deflected, this time into the gorge below. Again and again the protectors lashed out, and each time their bolts failed to hit anything or were sent skittering back to fry small groups of vorgs within the host that awaited. As quickly as the magical assault began, it stopped.

"Good girl, sis," Alan muttered. "You just take their wielders out of the action; let the others come to me."

A roar shook the narrow valley as the vorgs charged, many grasping the sides of long ladders as others stopped on the far side of the chasm to fire arrows up at the walls. Their siege engines rumbled forward at a slower pace.

"Fire!" Kron's bellow brought the archers atop the wall into action as arrow after arrow slipped from their bows to streak out of loopholes down into the mass of vorgs on the far side of the chasm. The thud and whir of the twin catapults as they launched their cargo of lumpy mayhem into the mass of vorgs was lost in the clamor of the incoming assault.

A handful of long ladders tilted upward across the chasm, packed with vorgs hanging from the rungs. Two ladders failed to land squarely, slipping off to the side down the fortress wall and tumbling into the depths below.

The three that held were all near the center of the wall, and vorgs raced up them. Within seconds two of these had been pushed away, sending their cargo screaming into the chasm. The last, however, wedged into a crenel, crushing one of Kron's archers against the stone, unable to move.

The vorgs surged forward, throwing themselves into the fight, where they were immediately cut down. From below, bolts from vorgish crossbows focused on the entry point, many taking their own warriors in the back, although several found their marks among the men struggling to free the ladder and push it away from the wall.

The next wave of ladders hit the wall, but of these, none managed to find purchase, either falling away on their own or pushed by Val'Dep warriors. The central battle at the top of the lone standing ladder intensified as vorgs climbed rapidly, most falling away as arrows from above cut into them, but some were gaining access.

Of Alan's platoon, only ten had bows, and these warriors also directed their fire at the vorgs climbing the ladder, although from their position on the northwest end of the fortress wall, the shots were long ones and had little effect. With a wave of his hand, Alan redirected his men's shots into the mass of vorgs jammed up on the far side of the chasm, where there was little opportunity to waste an arrow.

The vorgs threw more of the long ladders against the battlements, two going up beside the ladder stuck to the wall. The vorgs on those ladders grabbed hold of the other, lashing the three together. The men at the center of the wall converged to meet the vorgs trying to establish a hold at the top, and in that struggle, both men and vorgs tumbled outward and down.

Alan was beside himself with frustration. No ladders were being thrown against his far corner section of the wall as the vorgs concentrated on breaching the defenses at the center. Except for the archers among them, his platoon merely stood their ground behind the raised abutments and waited.

Again and again lightning rained down, trying to rupture the elemental shielding that Carol had erected above them. One of these forks ricocheted into the cliff high above Alan's position, sending a cascade of small pebbles and stones pinging down.

Three gruns, assisted by a large group of vorgs, pushed one of the giant siege engines close to the edge of the gorge. The gruns at the back of the machine began to turn the crank, lifting a six-foot-wide ramp of chained tree trunks skyward, angling it upward from the rear of the machine until it rose straight up a hundred feet into the air.

At its peak, the massive ramp wavered for a moment, and then it tipped forward, crashing into the top of the wall with such force that two of the protective abutments, behind which warriors waited, broke free, falling backward and burying the men beneath them.

A rush of vorgs scrambled upward as Kron ordered more men into the breach atop the wall. Kettles of boiling oil were poured down the ramp but did little more than cook the first wave of attackers.

In the center of the defenders, a bulge developed atop the wall as Kron struggled to divert more of his best fighters to the two spots where the vorgs poured upward.

Reloaded and cocked, the catapults whirred again, aiming for the spot where the siege engine braced the ramp on the far side of the chasm, but missing widely. The boulders bounded through the vorgs, but such were their numbers that the gaps refilled themselves almost as soon as the stones had passed.

Thick shafts of vorgish crossbow bolts clattered against the ramparts as the volume of fire from the far side increased. Although the slotted ramparts provided decent protection for the defenders, some shafts found their marks. The number of wounded and dying warriors of Val'Dep continued to rise at an alarming rate, thinning the ranks atop the wall.

A new wave of ladders fell against the wall in several spots near Alan's men, who leapt forward to dislodge them. Alan jumped up onto the rampart, bringing his ax down through the shield of the nearest vorg, cleaving his head from his body. His next swing shattered the right side of the ladder, which twisted away from the wall, sending its cargo tumbling into the depths.

"Alan! The center!" Bill yelled from his left.

A mass of vorgs had pushed their way onto the wall in the center of the line. The khan's warriors fought valiantly to push them back, but with each passing minute, more and more of the vorgs reached the top of the ramp.

Alan ran to the rear of the wall and waved his ax in a high elliptical arc. A set of flags echoed his signal across the line of women who worked behind the wall. Even under such circumstances, the sight of a couple of thousand women simultaneously throwing off their dresses was shocking.

All along the line, behind the walls, women in breeches and chain shirts ran to their prearranged spots, bows pointing skyward. The flag-bearers signaled again, and a high arcing stream of arrows winged their way up and over the wall, concentrated toward the center. As the women's nimble fingers worked the strings of their bows, nocking new arrows and firing as fast as they could, a buzzing like that of angry hornets filled the air.

Alan spun and raced back to the front of the wall just in time to plant his ax in the face of a vorg as his ladder fell forward into the crenel. Several grappling hooks sailed over Alan's head as the vorgs sought to secure the ladder from being kicked into the rift.

With a sweep of his ax, Alan severed the lines as Bill and two other soldiers pushed the ladder out and away, sending several dozen vorgs plunging to their deaths. One of his men staggered as a crossbow bolt stuck through his throat. Turning toward Alan, he tried to speak, but only a crimson froth appeared at his lips. His legs buckled, and he, too, plunged into the depths.

Across the wall to Alan's left, the storm of arrows was having an effect. Although many of them were falling short of the far side of the chasm, they rained down on the enemy climbing ladders, drastically reducing the numbers of vorgs reaching the top, allowing the khan's warriors to close the breach. Fighting remained fierce at the point where the ramp lay against the ramparts, but Kron's defenses now held.

The vorg attempts to breach other sections of the wall ceased as they pulled back out of bow range to regroup. Alan signaled the flag-bearers, and all but the center group of women archers stopped firing, although others continued to bring bundles of arrows up to the forward positions.

A yell from his left brought Alan's head around. Kron hobbled toward him so fast that he appeared to be hopping on his one leg, using the other as a short pole vault. Blood reddened his long braids and beard as it dripped from a scalp wound on the left side of his head.

"What is the meaning of this?" he bellowed as he neared Alan.

Alan's face showed no sign of emotion. "What are you talking about?"

Kron ignored Loraine as the chief matron arrived at Alan's side. "You know very well what I am talking about. Women acting like men, seeking to fight alongside warriors!"

"And doing a fine job of it, if you ask me," said Alan.

"I'm not asking you. Those women are wasting arrows by the hundreds. So many are falling short that we might as well be picking up the bundles and tossing them into the gorge. I've had three men seriously injured by shots misfired into our own ranks."

"Any time hundreds of archers are firing over lines in indirect support, some misfires happen."

"Archers? You call these untrained women archers?" Kron spun to directly face the chief matron. "And you, wench! You went along with this?"

"I did."

Kron swung the back of his gauntleted hand at her face, but it suddenly hit a brick wall as Alan's hand caught his wrist. The look of shock on Kron's reddened face, pulsing with fury, could not have been more explicit.

Alan moved forward until he was nose to nose with Kron. "Nobody strikes someone who is under my military authority, and you placed the chief matron and her women under my command."

Kron extricated his wrist from Alan's grasp.

"Fine. You want these women? Then you keep them. Get them out from behind my warriors. I would rather die with honor and glory than fight alongside women."

"And I would rather win in battle than lose," said Alan.

Kron sneered. "Mind what I said. Keep these wenches away from my lines."

With that, he spun on his peg leg and hobbled back toward the center of the wall.

"He's a fool," muttered Loraine.

"Yes, but he is in command, and you heard him," said Alan. "Chief, signal the women behind the center to cease fire and position all of your archers behind the western part of the wall."

The sturdy woman spat in Kron's direction, nodded, and turned down the ramp to carry out her instructions.

—ᴧᴧ—

The second charge came with a fury of noise. The beat, beat of vorgs pounding on their chests accompanied by their guttural roars built to a deafening chorus. High overhead the lightning storm once more descended upon Carol's shielding, and once again she scattered the blasts, although the noise shook the stone beneath Alan's feet.

A dozen ladders hit the wall near where he waited, as all along the ramparts the scene repeated itself. In answer, the lady archers of Val'Dep sent a concentrated storm of arrows arcing over Alan's men, cutting a ragged swath into the vorgs climbing toward them. The few that reached the crest along their section were cut down before they could climb over the ramparts, and once again, Alan's soldiers cast them into the depths.

"Alan, look," Bill yelled, pointing along the top of the fortress wall toward the center of the line.

The vorgs secured five new ladders to the ramp, giving a broad avenue to the vorgs and evil men who swarmed upward. At the top of the wall, the khan's warriors fought valiantly, but the vorgs pushed them steadily backward as more and more of their sparse numbers fell.

"Chief!" Alan yelled down to where Loraine stood. "Get some archers back toward the center and move your fighters up to take this section of the wall. The center is falling."

Without a word the chief matron spun away toward a flag-bearer.

"With me," Alan yelled, running toward where Kron now battled at the center.

Bill and the remainder of his men rushed after him, their positions immediately filled by women armed with ukeels, cleavers, and butcher knives. Another ladder landed, sending a pair of vorgs crashing into the pile of women. As Alan glanced back over his shoulder, the way the women swarmed over the vorgs reminded him of a pack of wolves pulling down prey. One vorg killed two of the women, but he was immediately pulled down as the others sliced at his ankles with ukeels and hacked and stabbed with cleavers and knives.

Running along the top of the wall, Alan shoved his way past old men and boys who manned intermediate positions, racing to get to the spot where the battle hung in the balance. Ahead, he spotted Kron, the warrior standing his ground against three vorgs, his hammer rising and falling as if he were at a smithy's anvil.

As he neared the rift in the line, Alan whirled his ax up and over his shoulder, sending a trio of vorgs tumbling backward to knock down several of their comrades.

The force of his attack spread the vorgs as he cut his way to the ramp. Behind him, his men pressed into the opening, killing invaders already on the ground and struggling to protect Alan's rear flank from those he had bypassed. The vorgs and brigands atop the wall faltered as they whirled around to see what had happened to those behind them.

Seeing their chance, Kron pressed his counterattack, driving forward with the twoscore warriors who remained alive and not so badly wounded that they could not fight. To Alan's left and right, his men struggled to clear away additional ladders.

Suddenly a stream of arrows arched overhead, picking up in volume as the women reestablished their firing positions behind the wall, cutting down on the number of interlopers making it to the top.

At the top of the ramp, Alan met the full force of the vorgs, arriving three to five at a time. Those that reached him died under his whirling ax, their brackish blood pouring off his armor. His arms bulged with effort until it seemed that they would snap the straps securing his armor. And indeed, one of his bracers burst and fell away.

Instead of being pushed backward, he waded forward through gore along a ten-foot section of the wall that held the mighty tree ramp, clearing away the vorgs that climbed it. A low moan rose up from the vorgs that were pressed forward into the savage terror who blocked the top. The moan built in volume, carried on the wind like the wail of a demon coming to collect the souls of the dead.

The sound sent a shudder through all who heard it, save that lone warrior, lost in the dance with his ax.

—៣—

"Lord Coldain, you should see this!" Roland called out from atop his horse on the crest of the hill.

Earl Coldain spurred his horse upward, the big bay scrambling up the shale of the hillside, its lungs working like a bellows. As he reached the side of his chief scout, he took the proffered far-glass. In the valley that led off to the northeast, a mass of several thousand vorgs was jammed up against a distant fortress. The outer wall of the fortress lined a deep chasm that stretched between the cliffs.

"How many would you say?" Coldain asked.

"Perhaps three thousand vorgs. It would appear they have one or more wielders with them, unless the weather around here is more unusual than expected. Take a look atop the wall."

Coldain held the glass to his eye, twisting it slightly to adjust its focus. All along the battlements, vorgs and a few humans clambered upward, although the bulk of the attack targeted the center. The defenders that fought atop the western third of the wall appeared to be women. The eastern third was not under direct attack. There, the chasm was widest, and a powerful waterfall plummeted down from atop the cliffs into the depths of the rift.

His trained eye showed him that the fortress was in dire trouble. The attackers had raised a massive ramp against the center of the wall over which vorgs surged upward. He trained the glass on the battle atop the ramp. Although twoscore men fought to either side of it, only one man held the top of the ramp.

Coldain fiddled with the glass, striving in vain for a better view. The vorgs surged forward in bursts, which the warrior cut down with a fury Coldain had never seen in all his years of battle. Between these rushes, the nearest vorgs shrank back until they were thrust forward by the press of those climbing behind them. And once again the slaughter commenced. For several minutes, Coldain watched the scene, unable to take his eyes from the struggle.

Turning to look back down the winding valley on the back side of the ridgeline atop which he now sat, Coldain could see the long lines of his own troops stretching into the distance, thirty thousand men strong.

All his life he had fought vorgs, killing them whenever the opportunity presented itself. Here he had run directly into a mess of them, set on the destruction of the men and women of a fortress city. He supposed he could put off tracking down and killing his old friend Jared Rafel for a couple of more days.

Earl Coldain glanced over at his chief scout. "How long do you think it will take to attack into the rear of the horde in that valley?"

"Two hours, if we push the men double-quick," said Roland.

"Halve that."

"You know there's no way that those people can hold that wall for that long," said Roland.

"At least we can avenge them. Tell my commanders to push the men like there's no tomorrow. For those people there won't be. I want all four of the wielders up here with me. And make sure Taras gets his ass up here first. Tell him I don't care how much he hates horses. Tie his butt to one if you have to."

Roland wheeled his horse into a gallop down the steep hillside.

Turning back toward the distant battle, Earl Coldain once again raised the far-glass to his eye. Atop the ramp, the lone warrior maneuvered his ax with a fury that Coldain could feel.

—∞—

Alan waded through gore up to his knees, kicking body parts aside as he struggled to keep his footing. The stench that wormed its way into his nose was rank. The unusual warmth of the midday air cooked the soup in which he battled.

Around him on the walls, women and men intermingled, struggling together to prevent the vorgs from gaining purchase as more and more of the ladders fell into place. The separation between the men's and the women's sections had long since disintegrated as the true desperation of the situation reached its peak. Very few of Kron's warriors remained alive to argue even if they had felt like doing so.

The women of Val'Dep poured up onto the wall from the rear, replacing their sisters as they fell. The losses that the vorgs inflicted on them appalled Alan more than any other part of the battle. Some of the beasts, upon reaching the top of the wall and encountering females, went into a frenzied state of rut, torn between rape and combat.

Often the former urge won out over their need for slaughter. Invaders grabbed women defenders from the front of the lines and passed them backward to the vorgs in the rear. While this was horrible to behold, the disruption it added to the vorgish attack aided the remaining women in killing those that they faced. That and the ferocity with which the sisters of Val'Dep struggled had prevented any breaches along the wall.

With each atrocity that he observed, Alan's battle madness grew, rage fueling his form so that he needed no rest. He wanted none. Once more, a rush of vorgs pressed forward into his whirling blade. He waded into them with renewed ferocity, his initial blow severing a shield and its wielder, descending in an arc that embedded it in the wood of the ramp itself. He twisted the ax to pull it free, but the handle broke, leaving the blade buried in one of the trees from which the ramp had been constructed.

Alan thrust forward with the broken shaft, driving it through another vorg as he grabbed the heavy war hammer from the dying man-beast's hand. Heaving the unfamiliar weapon, he sidestepped the thrust of a lance, swinging the hammer around in an arc that caved in the vorg's breastplate, rocketing him backward through three others, all of whom tumbled out and away into the chasm below.

A cool westerly wind swept the battlefield, forcing away the clouds that boiled overhead so that the sunshine broke through. Carried on that wind, the sound of hundreds of distant drums echoed from the canyon walls. An immediate change came over the army of the vorgs. The attack atop the walls faltered as those below spun to face a new threat. Over the shallow rise of the ridge, a league to the southwest, a host of men poured, moving forward in disciplined ranks, thousands strong. Fireballs arced through the sky to burst amidst the vorgs and brigands.

The vorgs broke and ran, fighting among themselves as they sought to escape back down the valley before this new army could close it off. With a yell, Alan charged, and behind him, the valiant sisters of Val'Dep and the surviving warriors raced after him.

In their panic, the vorgs dropped their weapons to run faster, but they were too late. The army of men sealed the escape route and then swept into them, cutting the warriors down methodically as the city's survivors nipped at their heels. Within two hours, the Battle of Val'Dep was over. No vorg, marauder, or foul priest remained alive on the battlefield.

26

Val'Dep
YOR 415, Mid-Spring

Alan raised his head to look about. The last of the vorgs before him
had departed for the land of the dead. Across the battlefield, he recognized the flags of the army of Tal, a sight he had never expected to
see again. He wondered who led the forces that his father had once
commanded.

A strong hand on his shoulder brought him out of his reverie. Kron
stood beside him, a lacerated mess, leaning on his war hammer as if
it were a crutch to compensate for his peg leg. The hardened warrior
looked at Alan strangely, scarlet dripping from the braids of his gray-
streaked blond hair and forked beard.

"They say you are the Chosen of the Dread Lord reborn, come
to this world to gather up comrades for a gathering war in the nether
realm."

"Well, you are of an age that you should know better than to listen
to idle chatter," said Alan.

"I know what I have seen this day."

The scars on the old trainer's forearms writhed like snakes as the heavy muscles in them clenched, emotion contorting his face. "All my life, I have wanted but one thing: to live and die a warrior. These last several years, after my leg was taken, I have felt less than a man, no longer deemed able to ride with the warriors. I was cast off to school the young men and boys, to make them what I no longer could be.

"How many times did I walk the wall, gazing down into the depths below, longing to throw myself outward and down? Too many to count. Yet I did not do it. Until today, I did not know why. Suddenly I have discovered why my destiny did not allow me to kill myself."

Kron's steel-gray eyes locked with Alan's. "You are the Dread Lord's Chosen. I knew it when I watched you hold the ramp. And at that moment, I knew my own destiny.

"I will be one of your comrades, following you until it is my fate to be sent onward to the nether realm, to fight alongside the Dread Lord. And if he does not accept me, then I will follow you anyway, that one day I may prove myself worthy of that honor."

Alan slowly shook his head but clapped a hand down on Kron's shoulder. "You're just as crazy as Bill, who's probably the one responsible for spreading these wild tales. But you're free to make your own choices. If you would follow me in this idiotic belief of yours, then so be it. I take no responsibility for your poor choices."

With a wild whoop, the older man moved with a quickness that belied his missing leg, wrapping his arms around Alan and slapping his back heartily. Then, leaning back, he extended his right arm, which Alan met with a forearm grip.

Kron grinned broadly, revealing the gap of three missing teeth newly broken off at the gumline, still oozing blood. "Then we have a pact. I am yours to the death."

"Seems like an idiotic pact, but I accept."

Over Kron's shoulder Alan could see Bill smiling. "Still alive I see," Alan said.

"So far so good," Bill replied. Blood dripped from the ranger's fist, indicating a wound higher up on the arm, but otherwise he seemed in reasonably good shape.

"Fine," said Alan.

He pointed toward a party of horsemen headed toward their position. "Well, gentlemen, it looks like we are about to meet our rescuers."

A company of riders trotted across the battlefield toward where Alan, Kron, and Bill stood, the lines of soldiers from the army of Tal parting to make way for them. In the lead rode a man that Alan recognized instantly, an imposing figure with armor that bore the crest of the house of Coldain.

Alan stepped forward as the riders came to a halt around them. "Earl Coldain. I hardly expected to see you again, but I must say that your arrival proved extraordinarily timely."

Coldain stared down at Alan in puzzlement. "Well, sir, you have the advantage on me. I don't recall meeting you before, even taking into account the prodigious amount of vorg blood that weeps from your body."

"It has been four years, and when last we met, you were no doubt focused on your conversations with my father, Jared Rafel."

The earl could not have looked more stunned if Alan had hit him in the face with the vorg war hammer he held. "Alan Rafel? The lad I remember bore little resemblance to the wondrous warrior who now stands before me."

Coldain swung down from his saddle, signaling the men with him to dismount as well. He stepped forward to meet Alan's outstretched arm in a strong grip. "There is certainly a good portion of your father in you. There is something else, too. I saw you hold that wall. I don't believe even Jared Rafel could have done that."

"Then you don't know my father as well as you think."

"He is the best leader of men I have ever known, and I have fought under his command in more battles than I care to count. Still, what I said remains."

Alan gazed out over the battlefield, where Coldain's soldiers had already begun piling the vorg carcasses into great mounds that they set ablaze. Only last year, the victory that had been won on this field today would have left Alan exultant. But now, the weight of the dead who had fought at his side constricted his chest until he struggled to breathe. The defenders of Val'Dep who remained alive gathered their wounded onto carts, the sounds of pain trailing away as the carts bounced across the rough road that led back toward the city.

The honored dead of Val'Dep would have to wait until those for whom life still lingered had been attended to. Alan did not even know what the custom among the khan's people dictated for treatment of the departed. There were so many, most of them women or old men and boys. There had not been many experienced warriors available for the defense when the battle started, and now almost all those were dead as well.

As he looked around, he also realized that only three of his soldiers remained: Bill and two others Alan hardly knew but who had fought exceedingly well, Thomas Franks and Charles Olwon.

All the rest had fallen. Only three left alive. Three of his thirty. Alan felt as though he was being buried, stiff, leaden, unable to walk. Once again, he had failed the men whom he led.

He pushed away the excuses that rushed in from the corners of his mind.

All dead.

All dead but three.

Curse of the Chosen

Seeing Alan's sullen gaze, Coldain stepped away, swinging back up onto his mount. "I understand your desire to tend to the needs of this fortress. My men will take care of the cleanup out on these fields. We cannot allow disease to spread from the rotting corpses. I will meet with you at sundown in my command tent, which I will have set up near the base of the vorg ramp. We have much to discuss, but it can wait until I have attended to more pressing affairs."

Alan turned back toward Coldain, his eyes regaining their focus. "There are actions that cannot wait."

"I am afraid they will have to. I have pressed my men hard to get here, and they deserve the rest that this night will bring. The people of this city have many more pressing needs of their own. No, Alan Rafel, our business together will wait until tonight."

With that said, Coldain whirled his mount around and galloped away, followed closely by his company of riders.

Alan watched him pass back through the lines of soldiers that awaited him. Then Alan turned and strode back toward the ramp that led up to the top of the outer wall, followed closely by Kron, Bill, and the others.

As Alan stepped out onto the top of the wall, the bustle of activity near him stopped as warriors, old men, lads, and women fell to their knees before him. The effect rippled out from where he strode, like a wave on a still pond, stopping him in his tracks. All around him atop the wall and spreading out across the broad grounds leading away toward the city, by the hundreds upon hundreds, the defenders of Val'Dep knelt before him.

Kron stepped up beside him and placed a hand on Alan's shoulder. "Chosen, they honor you, as do I." He dropped to one knee, head bowed.

Alan reacted angrily. "Get them up. Get them moving! I deserve no honor here. They should be honoring one another. They do me no service by letting the wounded wait while they kneel before me."

Kron rose to his feet and regarded Alan with a stern look. "Chosen, at a time like this, as much as during the heat of battle itself, people need a hero to look to, to make them feel worthwhile, to give themselves a sense of being a part of some larger struggle from which they have emerged victorious. You will do them no service by denying them that. Give them their moment before sending them back to their tasks."

Alan's gaze locked with Kron's for several moments. And then he nodded.

Stepping up onto a buttress atop the wall, Alan raised his fist, sending out a yell that echoed from the canyon walls. "Victory!"

"Victory!"

A tremendous roar erupted from the crowd as they rose to their feet. A dam of pent-up emotion erupted in a storm of noise that shook the walls of the city as the chant repeated itself, growing in volume with each chorus. The loudest chants of all came from Bill, Kron, and the rest of the survivors who had gathered on the wall behind Alan.

—∿—

In the canyon behind him, Earl Coldain sat on his horse watching the warrior standing atop the wall, fist raised toward the chanting people beyond. And as he watched, he felt the gooseflesh rise along his arms.

Beside him, Roland leaned closer to make himself heard. "That is a very dangerous young man."

The earl merely nodded.

—∿—

The evening air was cool, with an underlying dampness that clung to Alan's skin like drying blood. Cloying. The soldier leading him toward his meeting with Coldain did not seem to notice anything odd in the calm, but to Alan it crawled with portents of death.

How long had killing and death dominated his thoughts? What was it that had started this downward spiral? Not their flight from Tal. He had been happy on that long road, adventure lurking around every turn. It had not been when they established camp in the vale. He loved their peaceful valley more than any place he had ever seen.

No, it had started with the ranger mission. Since that time, those who dared serve with Alan died at a rate that no leader could find acceptable. Fifty percent losses would be considered devastating by any reasonable person. But those who dared fight alongside Alan Rafel suffered under a shroud of death where nine of ten died. Those deaths haunted him, the souls of the departed imploring him when he was able to sleep. Why had he let them down? Why could he not find an easier path to victory, as his father had always done? Tonight their blood wept onto his skin.

Atop the outer wall of Val'Dep, twilight was rapidly giving way to night, the deep purple in the west sinking to violet so dark that it was nearly indistinguishable from black. The crescent moon had risen above the eastern wall, its silvery presence casting enough light so that he could make out his path, although the outlines of the terrain faded in and out like poltergeists, belonging more to the spirit realm than to the earthly one.

Footsteps and a tapping from behind alerted Alan to the arrival of Kron, accompanied by Loraine. Alan stepped forward and took the chief's arm in greeting as fellow soldiers would do. The woman's eyebrows arched upward in surprise, and a grin split her lips, her teeth looking whiter in the semidarkness than they did in daylight.

"You never cease to surprise me, young lord."

"Nor you, me. You and your women acquitted yourselves superbly these last two days, true testaments of strength and strategy to rival the training of the finest of soldiers."

A harrumph from Kron brought a scowl to the chief matron's face. Kron cleared his throat, having some difficulty working himself up to speech. "Chief Matron, you know who and what I am."

"Yes. I accept the fact that you are our designated leader."

"No. I'm an old asshole. Have been for years. Not likely to change much at this point in my life, either."

Kron paused for a moment, clearing his throat once again before continuing. "But I am not such an ass that I can't admit when I have been shown to be wrong. Lord Rafel here has proven to be something that has given purpose back to my sorry existence. That rebirth of purpose has loosened the knot of bitterness that was strangling me.

"I feel as if I can breathe again. And with that breath, I can admit something that I could not have choked out a day ago. Without you and your women on the walls, Loraine, Val'Dep would have fallen. The Dread Lord's Chosen foresaw it and took the correct action."

"Dread Lord?" she asked.

"Would you quit spouting nonsense and get on with it?" said Alan.

Another harrumph escaped Kron's lips. "I am forced to admit that you, more so than I, were the effective leader of our people in this defense. That, along with my new destiny, leads me to formally transfer to you the title of acting steward and commander of Val'Dep."

Loraine's jaw dropped open. After several seconds, it snapped shut again. "What?"

"I have made up my mind to accompany the Chosen. I have pledged myself to him. To do that, I leave Val'Dep in your capable hands."

The chief matron turned toward Alan, who merely nodded. "Kron already discussed this with me, and I am in agreement. You are one of the most capable, steadfast leaders I have ever had the pleasure of meeting. But I must go, tonight. The time to save my people may already have passed, and I will wait no longer.

"You know what you must do. Gather the people together. Get the defenses of this wall reestablished. Although I believe we will hunt down and kill all of those who are responsible for the death and destruction here, you must prepare as if another attack will come against your walls tomorrow."

The steely look of determination on the chief matron's face reminded Alan of the first time he had met her.

"It will be done."

"Of that I have no doubt."

With that, he turned and walked down the ramp, moving in the wake of Coldain's escort, followed closely by Kron and Bill. As they made their way through the darkness toward the earl's camp, Alan marveled once again at how swiftly the one-legged warrior could move.

The sound of the flaps of Coldain's tent being thrown open ended Alan's reverie. He ducked inside, followed closely by Bill and Kron, who took up positions at his elbows. He paused just inside to allow his eyes to adjust to the bright light from the fire that blazed in the center, its smoke drifting up through the opening around the center pole some fifteen feet in the air. Loud laughter stilled at his entry, all eyes staring at the newcomer.

Coldain stepped forward and gripped arms with Alan, motioning him to a seat on the rug that covered the tent floor. A feast of venison, beans, and bread lay spread across the center of the carpet, and servers moved around the periphery, filling the glasses of those present from jugs of red wine.

Alan remained standing. "Earl Coldain. At your insistence, I have waited longer than reason should permit to broach a matter of critical importance. I have no time for feasting and drinking. I will wait no longer, despite my need for your assistance, which is great indeed."

A fleeting look of annoyance crossed Coldain's chiseled features. He turned to face Alan once more. "All right. I also have a matter of some importance, but I wanted to delay the moment of confrontation until I had allowed you a day of celebration of this victory. Now you force my hand."

Alan began to pace slowly back and forth before the earl, his jaw muscles clenching and unclenching repeatedly. Coldain's officers had stopped eating and had risen to their feet behind him.

"Look, while we are standing here making small talk and while your people are eating and drinking in celebration, my father, my sister, and my people are dying at the hands of the army that spawned the vorgs you helped us kill this very day.

"The force that came against us here is but a fraction of that horde. Just a day's march south of where we now stand, a battle is underway, and against such odds, I fear that even my father cannot prevail."

Coldain arched his eyebrows. "Alan, do you have any idea why I am here? Do you think I led the army of Tal all this way in the hopes that I could help your family in its escape from the edicts of the king?"

Alan's brown eyes glittered in the firelight.

"I was sent to arrest High Lord Rafel and his children and return all of you to Tal, where King Gilbert will put you on trial for high treason."

"And if we refuse to go?"

"Then the king has ordered me to kill you and return with your heads mounted atop pikes."

Alan felt his lips tighten into a thin line. "There are those who would say that you stand in a dangerous place to be making such threats."

"Of that I have no doubt. I do not tell you this to make threats. I tell you out of respect for your father and for the warrior whom I saw atop that ramp this morning. Jared Rafel has been my greatest friend since I served as his aide in the Vorg War.

"I was with him in Endar Pass when he courted Queen Elan. I was his best man at his wedding to your mother, Theress. I wept beside him at her funeral after she died giving you life. There is nothing in my heart that would drive me to hurt him except duty. I curse my duty with every waking now that it has come to this, but I am what life has made me. I will carry it out."

"I see you brought enough warriors to do the job. You must have over twenty thousand men with you."

"A few over thirty thousand, plus all the kingdom's wielders, except for Gregor, my wielder, Panko, and King Gilbert's pet, Blalock," said Coldain, his face grim.

"But that is madness. You have stripped Tal of its army in order to spend all these months chasing down one rebel lord. Even King Gilbert could not be such a fool."

"There is no limit to our young king's madness. He listens to his wielder's advice over that of his commanders. Once he made the decision, all argument was at an end. I spent more than a month gathering the army of Tal from my fellow lords.

"Since then I have pursued my oldest friend, sometimes losing the trail, but eventually regaining it. So, here I am."

A slow grin spread across Alan's face, stripping away the fatigue lines, a twinkle returning to his eyes. "Well, then, it is settled. We will need to make preparations for your army to move immediately."

Earl Coldain said nothing, a look of confusion on his face.

Alan spread his hands. "Surely you cannot permit a horde of vorgs and misfit priests to keep you from your duty by killing High Lord Rafel before you can arrest him."

The light dawned in Earl Coldain's eyes as laughter burst from his lips. All around the room, the tension broke as the laughter of his knights echoed his mirth. Coldain reached out, gripping Alan by the shoulders. "You are quite right. I cannot tolerate a deep-spawned horde killing one who deserves the honor with which I will engage him. I would see my old friend across a tall ale one last time before it comes to that."

Coldain wheeled toward his commanders. "Rouse the men. Have them ready to march by midnight. A good rest will have to wait for a couple of more days yet."

Turning back toward Alan, Coldain said, "Will you ride alongside me?"

"I would be honored. I will find you before midnight."

Swinging under the tent flap, Alan moved into the darkness, Bill striding beside him and Kron shuffling along in his wake. Alan would say his goodbyes to the people of Val'Dep before preparing for the ride. Those brave souls deserved nothing less. A specter of worry wafted around the corners of his mind at the thought of leaving them unprotected.

He dismissed the thought. Tomorrow he would fall upon their enemies, exacting a terrible toll for all those who had fallen. He only hoped that he would not be too late.

Seeing a shadow moving in the darkness to his right, Alan stopped. The form slunk back out of his sight.

"Who is that?" Alan asked.

"It's that woman, Katrin," said Kron.

"Katrin? Do I know her?"

"She was on the wall today. A tall, lanky girl, on the skinny side for my taste. For a woman, she fought very well."

Alan stared at Kron. For him to make that admission, she must have fought well indeed.

"What is she doing skulking around behind us?"

"She believes," Kron said.

"Believes what?"

"She saw what I saw, what we all saw. She believes that you are the Chosen. I told her to go away, but she will not. She intends to stay near you in the belief that she will prove herself worthy of acceptance into the army you are gathering for the realm of the dead. Fool woman."

Alan shook his head and resumed walking toward Val'Dep. "Well, then, she might as well tag along. She'll fit right in with this group."

The sound of Bill's glee followed him through the darkness.

27

Jared Rafel rubbed his forehead with the back of his hand, trying to clear away the blood that dribbled over his left eyebrow, blurring his vision. For the third time this day, the midfort, the next to last of his defensive positions, was about to fall.

This time there would be no stemming the tide that poured over the lower wall and into the narrow streets. A fireball burst into the watch-tower above and to the right of where Rafel stood, toppling it into the alley beyond, where the fire quickly spread to the log wall.

Rafel waved his arm in a hatchet motion, signaling men positioned all along the walls to break open the barrels of oil, loosing their contents to spill over the logs, the flammable contents quickly coating the wood and soaking into cracks and crevices.

He glanced up at the spire of rock where Carol and Kim remained. Carol's strength was undoubtedly failing. Some of the priests' attacks were getting through her defenses now, although she still managed to send forth a barrage of counterattacks whenever breaches occurred. She was weary, losing more focus with each passing hour despite Kim's aid.

"Fall back!" Rafel's yell rang off the walls as around him men struggled to comply as they fought the vorgs who were first into the alleys. A fresh volley of arrows from the walls behind cut into the vorg ranks, giving the retreating soldiers a small gap into which they ran. They hustled back toward the upper fort, the drawbridge of which was already beginning to rise. Rafel ran alongside them while the archers atop the wall did their best to provide cover until they were across.

As the last of his men crossed the bridge, it swung up, closing off access to their last defensive position. Across the flooded stream that boiled between the final fort and the one that had just fallen, the vorgs howled in anger and frustration. The volleys, launched by the bowmen atop the battlements, cut into the lead elements of the horde, driving them back behind the walls of the midfort, which they had just overrun.

Seeing Rafel's nod, Hanibal yelled an order to the archers. Within seconds, a wave of blazing arrows arced across the gap, embedding themselves in the oil-soaked logs of the fort just abandoned to the enemy.

Small fires quickly became big ones as the oil burned so hot that it ignited the logs themselves. The howls of the vorgs jammed up in the fortress became ever more desperate. They struggled to retreat from the inferno, but the mass of forces jammed up behind them made that impossible.

Thick clouds of smoke boiled between the narrow canyon walls, sending a choking pall spreading in all directions. Overhead, storm clouds loosed a deluge of rain as priests tried to quench the flames that swept through the midfort.

Across the river from Rafel's position, the hiss of steam as the water boiled off the burning logs accompanied screams as scalding vapors cooked all those within. A sudden wind howled down the canyon from the east, fanning the flames into a white heat and driving the steam back into the mass of vorgs inside the fortress.

A grim smile spread across Rafel's face. Carol was not done yet. The smile died away as he thought of his two daughters on the top of that rock, facing down dozens of the dark priests for days with no help. Where was Arn? He had never before failed Rafel. But this time he had. Perhaps the high lord had been foolish to think of Arn as invincible, but that was the image that had inspired the nickname Blade. He was more than the assassin who could not be stopped. He was the unbeatable legend. Until now. And that could only mean that Arn was dead. There was no other reason that he would leave Carol to wage a fight against such overwhelming odds as she had faced these last few days.

As he stared across the scene before him, a deep sadness settled onto Jared Rafel's shoulders, leaving them momentarily bowed. Then with a shake of his head, he strode back toward the center of his fort, yelling orders to his commanders as he passed.

It was time to extract a price in blood for what the protectors had done to his people, to his family.

—w—

Sitting on the ledge atop which Carol battled, Kim found that she could no longer find any nearby plant life to channel into her sister. Every tree, bush, or weed that had found purchase in the cracks of the rocks was now brittle in death. Exhaustion robbed her of the strength to do anything but place a hand on Carol's ankle, hoping that the knowledge that her sister was still beside her would lend some small comfort.

Kim found herself drifting into a dream, in which her brother's time-mist warriors ran swiftly across rough mountainous terrain. She was shocked to see that there were perhaps only three hundred, whereas Galad's command had numbered five times that.

The mist warriors flowed over the top of the ridge at a dead run, moving more gracefully than deer. They disappeared into the thick woods of the steep northern slope of a canyon. On and on they ran, climbing higher and higher up toward the head of the canyon.

As they neared the end of the canyon, two separate groups of vorgs ran along the tops of the ridgelines on each side of the canyon above the Endarians. Hundreds of the creatures raced to cut off the mist warriors before they could get out of the canyon and into the high forest beyond.

Now Kim could see what was slowing the Endarians. A large number of them were wounded, some so badly their fellow warriors carried them. To her utter dismay, Kim saw that one of these was Galad, his body hanging limply over the shoulder of Captain Tempas. Stifling a small cry, she opened her eyes to her own harsh reality.

—✴—

Jaradin Scot moaned as he struggled back to consciousness. Cramps racked his stomach, and the pounding in his head left him paralyzed. He could feel the cold, hard stone beneath the left side of his body, and try though he might, he could not uncurl from a fetal position.

He retched violently, although nothing but a foul taste was ejected from his stomach. His mouth felt like it was stuffed with cotton. His tongue felt like a piece of dried jerky. His remaining eye was so dried out that he was having difficulty focusing.

It was dark. Not a nighttime type of darkness. This was the darkness of a storm. A drop of water splattered on his brow, followed by a drenching downpour. Jaradin opened his mouth, letting the large drops fall inside. He swallowed, evoking a spasm of pain that brought sparks swimming across his blurred vision. Letting his cheek settle back down to the stone on which he lay, he licked at the small puddles forming in the chinks and hollows of the stone.

Brilliant flashes lit the ground as lightning forked overhead, followed immediately by thunder so close that it shook the stone beneath him. The wind howled around and below where he lay. Below? Where was he?

The sudden rush of memory rocked him. He had not dared to think about the dream in which Carol's voice had come for him, spiriting him out of the priest's body. He focused on his hand, pressed against the stone beside his face.

He flexed his fingers, turning the palm up so that he could see it. An old scar ran from the index finger along the life line of his palm, a scar he had gotten trying to cross a wire fence when he was six years old. Derek had been chasing him.

With supreme effort, he struggled to his hands and knees, although it cost him another round of retching spasms. These passed more quickly than before, leaving him shuddering but feeling a little bit stronger. Looking up, he could see that he knelt on a high shelf, a pinnacle of rock that jutted upward from the mouth of the canyon that led out of the vale.

Turning his body away from the edge of the precipice, he saw that he was not alone atop the pinnacle. Carol stood, her arms spread slightly from her body so that her hands angled out toward the canyon beyond, her eyes unfocused as she gazed into the storm.

Her brown hair clung damply to her pale skin, her white shirt heavily bloodstained. She was thin, dangerously so, and her lips were swollen and cracked. Jaradin wondered how long it had been since she had taken a drink of water.

Sitting by Carol's feet, clutching her leg, a slender Endarian woman knelt, her lovely face staring up at Carol with the same unfocused eyes. It seemed to Jaradin that he had never seen eyes that sad, as if the weight of the world tugged at the lady's soul. She had also clearly had nothing to drink in a very long time. Neither of the women appeared aware of his presence.

Looking around the ledge, Jaradin was shocked to see a pack with several full water flasks secured to its exterior lying just a few feet away from the two women. Crawling, slowly at first and then more rapidly as his muscles loosened, Jaradin reached the pack, removing and uncorking one of the flasks.

He tilted the container to his lips, letting a small amount of liquid trickle into his mouth, where he swished it around, testing for taste. It was water, maddeningly delicious water. He slurped down several gulps before forcing himself to stop, lest he vomit up what he had drunk.

Struggling to his feet, Jaradin stood panting, hands on his knees as the ground spun beneath him. Once the wave of vertigo passed, he staggered over to where Carol stared out into space, carefully tilting the jug of water to her lips, letting a trickle of water spill into her mouth.

Involuntarily she gulped twice, her eyes clearing before her focus returned, once again, to the task on which she concentrated. Jaradin continued pouring small portions of water between her parted lips, which she swallowed, although she did not again lose focus on her task.

Kneeling down, he repeated the process with the Endarian woman, who also managed to take several swallows from the flask. When she ceased swallowing, Jaradin tilted the jug back to his lips, allowing the wonderful liquid to wash down his throat.

Setting the jug down near Carol, he turned to walk toward the edge of the pinnacle. After two steps his knees buckled so that he fell to his hands hard enough to bring blood to his skinned palms. From the fire in his knees, he doubted that they had fared much better. Crawling the remaining few feet to the edge, he seated himself so that he could look down on the canyon below.

A stunning scene confronted him. Clearly the forces of High Lord Rafel had been hard at work building new fortifications the several months that he had lain rotting in his dungeon cell. Most of those fortifications now lay in the hands of the army of the protectors.

A horde filled the bottom of the ravine, crowded up against the spot where High Lord Rafel's soldiers held out in the last of his canyon forts.

A pall of smoke continued to drift from a fort that the vorgs controlled, although it was so badly damaged as to be of no use to anyone now.

The battle centered atop the walls of the final fortress, perched across the entrance to the expanse that was Areana's Vale. Vorg ladders and ramps formed a nearly continuous latticework that stretched across the flooding mountain river to the top of thirty-foot-high log walls.

Several ten-foot-tall gruns had managed to wade through the raging current of the rapids, holding on to one another in a bizarre parody of a royal dance. On their shoulders they held another large ramp, which was shielding them from the arrows and other projectiles raining down from atop the fortress wall.

Jaradin was surprised to see a formation of several hundred horsemen positioned out in the open valley of the vale, waiting in reserve should the upper fortress be breached. He had no memory of who these horsemen were, but their appearance reminded him strongly of the Kanjari, Ty.

After several seconds he recognized the barbarian among the horsemen, standing out as the only one who rode bare-chested. As for soldiers, there was no sign of any additional backup, Rafel having apparently already committed his foot reserve to the fight.

As Jaradin watched, the fighting in the fort below became ever more desperate. With each passing minute, it became more apparent that this would be Rafel's last stand. Jaradin could make out no more than a couple of hundred soldiers left fighting inside.

Even counting the several hundred barbarian horsemen who awaited their chance to get into the fight, the defenders were outnumbered at least ten to one by the forces jammed into the lower sections of the canyon. Fireballs and lightning rained down from above, although these struck a shimmering shield that sent them ricocheting off into the canyon, making the rock walls vibrate like the skin of a drum. The sound was as painful to his ears as the stench of ozone and sulfur was offensive to his nose.

Jaradin longed to make his way down to stand beside his comrades in the last defense of the vale. But he could barely stand. Climbing down the steep trail that wound its way to the top of the pinnacle was out of the realm of possibility.

He looked around at the women occupying the ledge, the two looking frail and vulnerable despite the aura of power radiating from Carol. When had they last received food or rest? From the evidence of their water deprivation, Jaradin was amazed that they were conscious. As he watched, three drops of blood seeped from Carol's left eye, carving a trail down her cheek.

A sudden resolve settled over Jaradin Scot. She had rescued him from a pure form of torture. Even if that rescue meant that he was soon to die at the hands of a pack of foul beasts, he blessed the ground on which she stood.

Cutting off a piece of his shirt, Jaradin carried one of the water jugs back over to the women. Soaking the rag, he began gently bathing Carol's face with the cool, damp cloth. Although the gesture might be meaningless, he would stay here and provide what care he could to ease her physical distress. He owed her that at least.

—m—

From his position in a tower at the rear wall of the fort, John worked his bow with a steady rhythm. Nock arrow, select target, fire, repeat. He was deeply grateful for the excellent prepositioning of arrows that left him with a limitless supply in each of the spots where he worked his abilities. He did not doubt that this would be his final stand, wishing that he could at least have said farewell to Kim.

There was nowhere to go but the valley from here, and that was no place for an archer. When the vorgs broke through this last line to the vale beyond, they would be in Ty's realm. In the meantime, John would do his best to deplete their numbers.

How long had it been since he had been in the possession of hope? An hour, perhaps? An arrow from the rangers on the rim had carried the message that the army of Tal was attacking into the vorgs from outside the canyon.

But the horde of vorgs and priests clearly had a driving hope, and that was to force their way through Rafel's smaller numbers, setting up their own defenses from within Areana's Vale.

In desperation, the vorgs and marauders threw themselves at the walls of the upper fort, backed by the wielding of their priests. While John was thankful for Carol's protection from the mystical attacks, it kept her from counterattacking in a way that they desperately needed. Now the horde was within the fort itself, and its fall could not be long off.

A yell from John's left accompanied the tower tilting wildly as it sagged on its supports. Its fall threw him against the braces. He clawed his way back to his knees, spitting out blood and teeth. Scrambling along the tilted floor of the tower, he found that it had not fallen to the ground but lay braced against an abutment atop the wall. A twenty-foot-wide section of the east wall had collapsed, and through it hundreds of vorgs poured into the vale.

A wild cheer arose from the invaders, a yell matched by the hundreds of horsemen who charged forward in a column of threes, bows in hand. The vorgs set up a line of pikes to meet the charge of the khan's cavalry, but the horsemen wheeled around before the pikemen. Loosing volley upon volley of arrows into the vorgs, they mowed them down. Despite the heavy losses, the horde continued to pour through the hole in the outer wall.

John realized the target of the attack. While more vorgs raced to fill the gaps in the line of pikemen, a number raced south, aiming for the steep trail that led up to the top of Carol's pinnacle. Seeing that none of the horsemen realized what was happening, John spotted Ty readying his ax for the charge. John climbed out the window of the tower, waving his arms and shouting, but his efforts to attract attention were lost in the din.

In desperation, John angled his bow high into the air, loosing an arrow in Ty's direction. It streaked outward and down, embedding itself in the bone shaft of Ty's ax.

The barbarian's head spun in John's direction. Seeing his friend waving and pointing, Ty swiveled his gaze to the group of vorgs that had almost reached the pinnacle's base. The Kanjari charged, lying low across his palomino stallion's back.

The speed with which the horse ran was beyond what John would have imagined possible. Seeing the lone rider bearing down on them, the vorgs near the pinnacle braced spears and pikes against the ground, tips pointed outward toward the charging rider.

John launched arrows so rapidly that his bowstring sounded like a lute. Each arrow arced outward into the head or neck of one of the vorgs toward which Ty and his stallion hurtled. The stallion jumped as it neared the outer line of vorgs, and for a moment it appeared that the forest of spears would impale it.

In an acrobatic miracle, Ty leapt forward over the stallion's neck, his crescent-bladed ax severing the shafts of those spears in his direct path. The horse's flying hooves caved in the skulls of the disarmed pikemen. Ty's body cartwheeled across the ground as his shoulder struck the earth.

"No!" John's yell did not slow his bow, and an arrow caught the throat of a vorg that tried to impale his friend. Another vorg dashed in with a long curved knife to cut Ty's throat. Scrambling to a knee, Ty caught the vorg by the arm with one hand and grabbed the man-beast's armor with the other. With a tremendous effort, he lifted the vorg above his head, rising from his knees to stand in the same motion. More of the vorgs charged but were bowled over as Ty tossed their flailing comrade into their midst.

Righting himself, Ty slapped the rump of his stallion, sending it racing up the trail toward the top. Then he turned with his ax, setting it into a blur, severing limbs from the bodies of the vorgs trying to get past him. The warriors who did not fall to his ax sprouted feathered shafts as John worked his bow, and though the pile of bodies grew ever deeper, the press of vorgs toward Ty continued unabated.

—⁓—

From atop the toppled tower, the volume of sound coming from John's bowstring grew so loud that soldiers throughout the fort turned their heads to catch what they thought was a distant minstrel's tune, wafting above the sounds of war.

It harmonized with the percussion of clashing metal, the wails of the dead and dying, the calls of young men for their wives or mothers, and the guttural growls of vorgs. The sounds formed a symphony so macabre that old Gaar, blood running freely from a wound in his thigh, began to cry. Once again focusing, he slashed with his sword and then kicked the headless body of a vorg from the high wall.

28

Northwest of Areana's Gorge
YOR 415, Mid-Spring

Alan, astride his warhorse, crested a rise at Earl Coldain's side, pulled forward by the sight of the mass of vorgs and brigands jammed up at the entrance to the gorge that led to the vale. Clouds piled above the cliffs, webs of lightning crawling through them. The trailing edge of the enemy army lay no more than a half league from where Alan impatiently sat atop his mount.

"Steady now," said Coldain from Alan's right. "First we soften them. Then we strike."

Alan understood the tactic, but the tension that this period of waiting put into his muscles was almost unbearable. He looked around at the infantry that marched along the back side of the ridge, swinging wide to cut off the vorg army from retreating to the west. The main attack would have to wait just a bit longer before these brigades were in position.

"Call forth my wielders," Coldain commanded.

A signalperson raised a red flag high, then slashed it downward to point directly at the massed vorgs and brigands. Coldain's four wielders stepped into their positions along the top of the ridge, separated from one another by a dozen paces. Taras, his brown robe draping his rotund body, stood to Coldain's right. Farther to the west, Lektuvu, a petite wielder with spiked blonde hair, stood resplendent in her gleaming silver robe. Beyond her right hand, stroking his trimmed gray beard, stood Vanduo, robed in turquoise. Gaisras, a redheaded wielder of motherly build, stood last in the line, her bright orange robe seeming to pull flame from the air.

As if in response to Alan's last thought, Gaisras extended both hands, and a fireball the size of a wagon wheel arced outward toward the distant enemy, leaving the smell of brimstone in its wake. It smote the ground in the midst of the unsuspecting horde, bounding three times.

Lektuvu clapped her hands, then threw them wide, summoning a wind that howled out of the east, fanning the blaze into a brilliant torch that cut a swath through the vorgs.

For several moments, Alan thought that the protectors might be too surprised to offer an effective defense. But when they did respond, the raging fireball winked out of existence, and lightning crackled across the sky toward the new threat. Lektuvu swept her right hand in an arc, and the first bolt of lightning deflected off a shimmering shield of air. Then Taras spoke a single word as he pointed forward. "Sausumos."

Alan's hair flared out as if he had rubbed his head with a rag as the remainder of the protectors' lightning was diverted to a distant mound of earth, multiple bolts striking the same spot. The crackle of the strikes was immediately drowned out by a crash of thunder that hurt Alan's ears. As if on cue, Vanduo turned his cupped palms to the sky, then appeared to empty their invisible contents on the ground. A curtain of rain dropped from the distant clouds to obscure the vorg army.

Then the earl rose in his stirrups and bellowed the command that Alan had been awaiting. "Charge!"

Feeling a surge, Alan spurred his warhorse forward, accompanied by the thunder of Coldain's cavalry.

—m—

Jorthain raged. To have defeat snatched so swiftly from the jaws of victory was something he could not fathom. How could his god have failed him so miserably? The deep take its cursed, festering flesh.

He stood in the midst of the remains of his army, trapped between the massive force that had come from nowhere to squeeze him into this canyon and the accursed horsemen who were preventing what was left of his horde from escaping into the valley beyond. He gazed up at the ghostly witch standing atop the rock escarpment several hundred feet above. He summoned a boiling gout of power that lashed out at her. The effect was the same. Nothing. Blocked.

By the dark gods, if he were going to die, at least he would take her with him.

A fireball crashed into the cliff fifty feet above his head, creating a shower of debris. Fury filling his veins, Jorthain hobbled over and grabbed Hargin, an aged priest who cowered before his gaze. "What in the deep was that?"

Hargin's panic pulled a long wad of spittle from his slack jaw. "Master, I'm sorry. We were trying to do a casting to aid your army against the horsemen when the wielders from outside interrupted us."

"I don't care about the safety of those vorgs. I told you to keep the wielders off my back, and I meant it, you fool. The next time any of you fail to obey me, I will have your guts for a necklace. Get it done."

As Hargin scrambled back to the group of priests, Jorthain walked to where a huge vorg stood gazing toward the breach in the fort's east wall.

Jorthain tapped the warrior firmly with the knobbed end of his bone staff. "General Jerg! I thought I said I wanted that bitch taken from the top of that pinnacle. Why am I still standing here waiting?"

The vorg's red eyes squinted down at the high priest. "There has been a complication."

"A complication? I thought you said there was only one man holding the trail."

"There still is."

"And you haven't killed him? Why is it taking so long to drive him back?"

"He's driving us back. I'm having a hard time pushing my vorgs forward at him."

"What?" The high priest's voice rose until it was nearly a scream.

"To kill that man, I would have to pull more men from the attack against the horsemen."

"And you hesitate? Kill him. Don't talk to me about horsemen. I want that man dead. I want that path cleared. Now."

The commander turned away, cursing and tossing vorgs aside as he strode toward his other commanders.

Jorthain followed, a dull ruby aura surrounding him, pushing all who impeded his progress out of his way. Arriving at the broken-down east wall, he moved through the gap, stepping up into an area where the rubble sheltered him from attacks from the remainder of the men who fought atop the ramparts.

From this vantage point he could see the fighting at the base of the trail as it wound between boulders. The fighting moved in rushes and waves as the vorgs threw themselves at the warrior who blocked their way.

Despite their superior numbers, they were being swept aside in a way that would have been frightening if Jorthain had been capable of such a feeling. The demon with the ax moved as if he were dancing, a dance that must have brought rapture to the gods of violence.

He wasted no motion. A dodge became a whirling cut that severed torsos. One step back coiled him for a strike that thrust him three steps forward. The vorgs nearest to the warrior cowered back until they were thrown forward by those behind them. Their moans of dread rose, making their way to Jorthain's ancient ears.

Suddenly he sensed what he had been waiting for. The sudden, coordinated attack of his priests had distracted the witch as she lashed out in a counterstrike against them. Ignoring the cries of his priests as they died, Jorthain seized the brief opening in her defenses, wrapping the warrior who swept his army from the path in chains of elemental strength.

A wave of exaltation swept through the high priest as he saw the warrior freeze, his ax raised high above his head, muscles knotted in effort but unable to bring the weapon crashing down into his foes.

With a roar, a huge vorg lunged forward, driving his spear through the warrior's stomach and then grabbing both ends where it had passed through the man, lifting him off the ground on the impaling shaft.

The glory of the moment proved short-lived as Jorthain felt a furious presence fill his head. "Not possible!" he thought as the witch's mind filled his own, ripping the fabric of his consciousness from its moorings in the gray matter of his brain.

The witch's mind clawed at his, shredding his sanity as thoroughly as his dark god had done to some of the high priest's human sacrifices. By the time she finished, there was not enough left of Jorthain's mind to power his heart, much less his legs. An empty shell toppled limply forward, to rise no more.

—⚬—

Alan listened to the thunder that rumbled overhead as Coldain's four wielders hammered into the defenses thrown up by the protectors. The columns of the earl's soldiers stretched to the horizon, the lead elements having swung wide to cut off any retreat by the horde that they now encircled on three sides. The ferocity with which they had struck into the vorgs had stunned and panicked the enemy, driving them up against the cliffs that framed the gorge that led to Areana's Vale.

So far, Alan had avoided combat except to cut down any who tried to block his path. He had abandoned his horse so as to draw as little attention as possible and thus raced along the south flank of the vorgs. He entered the canyon into which they crowded, staying as near as possible to the south wall.

Startled vorgs saw him pass among them, barely having time to yell before he disappeared through the crowd. Those that were quick enough to attack him died violently, failing to slow his progress.

The canyon thrummed with noise, giving the impression that the walls would give way at any moment, sending a cascade of lumpy death plummeting down on all crowded within. Alan gulped in great quantities of air that stank of blood and smoke. His passage was made easier by the vorgs' focus on advancing deeper into the canyon, anxious to break through the last of his father's defenses.

The concern that drove Alan ever faster was the thought that he was already too late. That worry grew as he forged his way through the vorgs that crowded the wreckage of the lower forts, which they had overrun and burned. The confusion within the ravine aided him, the smoke making it more difficult to identify him as different from the men who were a part of the army of the protectors.

The sight of vorgs flowing into the last fort made him feel as if he had been kicked in the pit of his stomach. As despair flooded into him, he saw that men still fought atop the walls, although a rupture along the east side had opened into the vale. Through that gap Alan could see the horsemen of the khan counterattacking.

A glow from above brought his attention to the figure clad in billowing white who stood with her arms outstretched atop a pinnacle of stone. Carol. The knowledge that his sister had remained up there without rest since before the Battle of Val'Dep had started put a lump in his throat. How could she defend them all for so long against that many wielders?

As his gaze came back toward the ground, a tightness in his chest momentarily stopped his breathing. A large group of vorgs was struggling to clear their way to the path that led up to where Carol stood. Blocking their way, a lone figure battled—Ty.

A low rumble built inside Alan's chest, erupting as a roar as his racing feet sped him toward that spot. A trio of vorgs saw him and jumped to block his passage. The force of the blow from the hammer he wielded caved in the head of the first, burying parts of the skull into the chest of the second. Alan's flying momentum carried him into the third with such power that his shoulder lifted the vorg, sending him spinning away through the air.

The vorgs around Ty were so heavily engaged that they failed to notice Alan's arrival until too late. He tore into their backs with a hammer in one hand and a sword in the other.

Caught between the two titans of battle, the remaining dozen vorgs hesitated in their confusion, a hesitation that merely sped their passing to the nether realm. Ty's grand ax swept around one last time, dispatching the last of the vorgs.

Alan spun to see what other enemies might be following, but found that none had made it around the side of the rock spire to where the sheltered trail disappeared within the boulders. As he looked back, Ty staggered, pitching face forward onto the stone, his ax sliding from his fingertips to clatter to the ground several feet away. Alan rushed to his side, propping him into a seated position against the stone wall. In horror, he saw that Ty was grievously injured. A jagged hole gaped in the center of his stomach.

"Aaahh . . ." The sound escaped Alan's lips before he could clamp them shut.

The barbarian grinned feebly before erupting in a fit of wet coughing that splattered Alan with more blood. Ty's head turned, and his arm stretched out in the direction of his ax, unable to reach it. Alan jumped to retrieve the weapon and placed it in Ty's hand.

The Kanjari clutched it to his chest with both hands, a broad smile once more on his lips. "Glorious."

The word rasped from Ty's mouth as his steel-blue eyes shone with a savage light. He reached a hand out to clutch Alan's wrist, the power of the grip threatening to break bone.

"I'll await you on the other side. When I have made the crossing, let no other touch my ax. I want you alone to use it. You can return it when we meet again. Do I have your word?"

"You have it."

Alan gripped Ty's face in his hands so that he looked directly into the barbarian's eyes. "I am so sorry that I was late arriving. If I had only been here a little sooner . . ."

Ty's lips moved, but with the words on his lips only half formed, the light in those savage eyes went out.

And as the Kanjari who had saved both his and Carol's lives died in his arms, Alan's yell of despair echoed from the cliffs.

29

Areana's Vale
YOR 415, Mid-Spring

High Lord Rafel and Earl Coldain stood together on a rocky promontory, gazing over the broad expanse of Areana's Vale. The smoke from the huge pile of vorg carcasses billowed up in thick greasy plumes, its stench swept from the valley by the early morning breeze.

Neither Rafel nor Coldain had granted mercy to their enemies. The army of Tal had killed every marauder, vorg, and grun on the field, piling their carcasses to build the bonfire that yet burned.

The army had suffered thousands of casualties, but the remaining troops had set up a series of encampments that stretched for leagues through the vale. Except for a rare few, including their leader, that massive army still slept.

Clapping a hand on Coldain's broad shoulder, Rafel led the way back to his council chambers, which had miraculously remained undamaged during the battle that had wrecked the upper fort around it. The captain of his guard snapped to attention as the two leaders passed through the thick door. As the two men seated themselves near the flaming hearth, Rafel leaned back and grinned at his friend. "James, you have an excellent sense of timing. I never thought I would get the opportunity to see you again."

Coldain spread his hands. "It was a pleasure to once again serve alongside you. I wish it could last."

"Ah, yes. I wondered at that. Alan has enlightened me about your mission. I can't say that I'm surprised. I guess the only surprising thing is that King Gilbert had enough sense to send you instead of having you killed before he could take advantage of your sense of duty."

"It came as a bit of a surprise to me, too."

Coldain leaned back in his chair, clasping his hands behind his head. "Still, there's no point in rushing into the unpleasantness," he said. "Perhaps we could spend a day to honor all the heroic dead and let the people celebrate their victory before that. I would dearly love to spend an evening in feast and drink with my oldest friend."

Rafel nodded. "I would like that. Although it is traditionally the responsibility of the host, I would appreciate it if you prepared the festivities. I have a long day ahead of me, sharing the grief of the widows and children of the men who died in my service. It is such a little thing to sit for a while and hold their hands while they weep. They deserve at least that much.

"At sunset, I will have my high priest, Jason, conduct the Ceremony of Farewells. Then I would very much enjoy spending an evening getting deep in the cups with you."

At that moment, the captain of the guard entered the room. "Sorry to interrupt you, High Lord. Two riders have arrived, and they insist upon seeing you immediately."

"Insist?" Rafel let his irritation bleed into his voice.

"Yes, sir. The insistent one is Blade."

The high lord's jaw dropped. "Well, what are you waiting for? Let them in."

Arn strode into the room, gaunt and unshaven, accompanied by a distinguished lad who seemed vaguely familiar to Jared Rafel.

With an exclamation, Coldain leapt to his feet and raced forward, throwing his arms around the young man, embracing him in a hug that threatened to crush the life from him. The youth returned the embrace, kissing Coldain firmly on the cheek. "Good to see you, Father."

Recovering his composure, grinning from ear to ear, Coldain turned to Rafel. "Jared, you remember my son, Garret, don't you?"

Rafel stepped forward to grasp wrists with Garret Coldain. "I hardly recognize you, you've grown so. It's good to see you again, son."

"And you," said Garret.

"Come sit down," said Rafel, directing them toward the table. "Captain, could you have some food and drink prepared and sent over? Servings for four."

"Yes, sir."

The captain vanished, closing the door behind him.

Rafel extended his hand across the table to Arn, who took it firmly. "I didn't think you could surprise me after all these years, but you somehow managed it."

"Glad to be around to do so."

Earl Coldain leaned forward, elbows on the table, concern creasing his brow. "Okay, Garret. How and why are you here? I left you in charge of our estate. What has happened?"

For the next hour, interrupted only slightly by a hearty breakfast, Garret laid out the tale that had sent him on the journey in search of his father.

He told of how Blalock in reality was Kragan, who, having stripped the kingdom of its defenses, brought in a mighty host of vorgs and men who were set loose to destroy all that had been the kingdom of Tal. He told of how Kragan, having no further need of the king, had murdered

Gilbert and then set about killing every remaining nobleman in the kingdom. Only freak luck had saved Garret from a similar fate.

He had been knocked unconscious and washed down a storm drain as Kragan's army overran the Coldain estate. Having come to in darkness, he had dug his way out of the pile of wood and plaster to find that he was the only person left, the others having been slain or taken away into slavery. Garret told of how he had discovered his mother's tortured and burned body within the keep and how he had been unable to find his little sisters.

This pulled from Earl Coldain a howl of sorrow and anguish that rattled the door. His fist hammered the table, bloodying the knuckles of his right hand. Only after the earl had calmed himself did Garret continue his tale in a husky voice.

Torn by grief, Garret had determined to find his sire and the army of Tal so that a debt of vengeance could be brought home to the wielder Blalock. The journey to find his father had been long. Many times he had lost the trail and had been forced to backtrack or sweep around in a wide arc before coming across word of the large force moving to the west and then north.

Garret leaned back in his chair, pushing away his plate and wiping his face on his sleeve. "At the end it would have all come to disaster if not for the arrival of Blade."

Garret glanced over at Arn, who had also finally eaten his fill. "My horse had gone lame, and a party of twenty vorg guards was on my tail when he began appearing, coming and going along the route, each encounter lessening the number of vorgs who pursued me. Three of the vorgs finally had me cornered atop a small rise after my horse died, and it looked like I would not be finding my way to you. Then Blade introduced himself to them.

"Growing up, I always thought Blade's reputation was overblown. How wrong I was. Blade was as surprised to see me as I was to see him, but it was a mutually agreeable encounter. So I hopped on the back of his horse, and he brought me back here. It seems that we missed all the action, though."

Rafel watched as the elder Coldain reached across the table and gripped forearms with Arn. "Thank you for saving my son's life," the earl said, his ravaged eyes shining with moisture. "And for returning him to me. All these months I have spent in useless pursuit. I allowed myself to be used, a mindless slave to my duty, a pawn used to strip the kingdom of its defenses. As glad as I am to see Garret, his foul news sickens me to my core."

Earl Coldain rose to pace the floor. "I will not let Kragan's treachery go unpunished, nor will I let the army of Tal go to waste. I will make him pay for what he has done to those I love."

"And I will help you," said Rafel, working hard to tamp down his own fury. "But it won't hurt us to take time to plan our response before acting. In the meantime, I propose that we continue with our original plan for this day. Let me lend what comfort I can to those of my people who have suffered unbearable loss, and then we will feast over a great mutual victory so that our people's spirits may be uplifted. Tomorrow will come."

A leaden Earl Coldain walked over to his son and placed an arm over the young man's shoulders. "Agreed. First, we honor this victory. We will leave vengeance for another day."

Coldain started toward the door with Garret, then paused, turning back to where Rafel sat beside Arn. "An army can only have one leader."

Rafel slowly nodded.

Coldain continued, "I have served under your command since the Vorg War, have learned everything I know about combat and leadership under your tutelage. I see no reason to change that hierarchy. Tomorrow, I will inform my commanders of my pledge of fealty to you. Tonight, though, I will end my command of the army of Tal with a feast, the like of which has not happened in many a year."

Then he turned and departed.

After they had gone, Arn stood to face Rafel, his face a mask of deep emotion. "The captain of the guard told me a bit of the battle on the way up. Since Carol is resting, would you mind showing me to the spot where Ty fell? I would like to pay my respects to my friend. Then I will go sit by my fiancée until she awakens."

As they walked out into the courtyard, the Scot brothers rounded the corner with Derek's black bear, Lonesome, ambling along behind. Rafel shook hands with each of the rangers, noting the improvement in Lonesome's attitude toward Jaradin. "Good to have the real you back, Jaradin. Carol has already told me of your ordeal."

Jaradin met his gaze. The ranger's bold spirit shone in his face despite the scars and his missing eye. "Glad to be here."

Derek clapped a hand on his brother's back. "And I'm relieved to see that Jaradin isn't the slacker I thought he'd become."

"You'd think," said Jaradin, "that my own brother might be a little more observant than to believe that an evil priest inhabiting my body is just me with a bad attitude."

"Yeah, well, I've never seen you in love, now have I?" said Derek. "I thought maybe that was just how it affected you."

Jaradin shook his head. "I also wanted to pass along my heartfelt thanks to your daughter," he said. "I have already told her, but I wanted to let you know as well. What she did to save me is more than I can ever repay, but I will try."

"I'm sure she knows that."

As Rafel watched the Scot brothers depart, Arn turned toward his mentor. "That daughter of yours has an interesting effect on all those around her."

"You don't say. Now let me show you where Ty saved our girl."

Stepping out of the building, he led Arn toward the pinnacle. As they walked out through the ruins of the upper fort, the high lord felt his deep sense of loss return. So many of the people he loved had given their lives so that friends and family could continue to live.

His anger at all that Kragan had wrought lurked just beneath the surface of that sadness, but Rafel would bank that battle fury for later.

30

Endar Pass
YOR 415, Late Spring

Galad led his more than three hundred warriors out of the time-mists that draped the entrance to Endar Pass. His mother, Queen Elan, stood at the front of several thousand Endarian warriors, waiting to greet them. Dressed in a turquoise gown, her raven hair cascading down her back, she looked like a goddess. While he would normally have been happy to see her, there was now no room for happiness in his heart.

As he approached, Elan signaled with her hand, and several life-shifters hurried forward to assist with the wounded. It was an act that Galad welcomed, having lost his last two life-shifters during their retreat to Endar Pass.

Since the mist warriors needed rest and recuperation, Queen Elan kept the welcoming ceremony mercifully short. Then she invited Galad into her carriage for the ride back to her palace. It was not a ride that he had looked forward to.

"I am sorry, my queen, for the defeat that I suffered on the battle-field," Galad said after they had gotten underway.

"Nonsense. You and your warriors bought us precious time that I've put to good use, summoning warriors from throughout Endar. They have already begun to arrive."

A tightness in Galad's chest made it difficult to speak of those that he had lost. "At the cost of more than a thousand of our precious mist warriors."

The queen sighed and placed a hand on his arm. "You blame yourself for something that I ordered done, knowing that perhaps none of you would return from this mission."

Elan paused, catching his gaze. "The runner you sent to alert me to your return told of how you wielded the mists while leading your warriors into battle."

"With Laikas dead, I had no choice but to take that risk."

Saying his dead lover's name brought the memory of her body flooding back into Galad's mind. His face felt numb.

"Ah, Laikas," Queen Elan said, her expression becoming somber. "I am so sorry for your loss, my son."

Galad stared out the window as the carriage crossed the white bridge that linked the lake's southern beach with the ivory fortress and island city that lay beyond. The azure water sparkled beneath the midday sun, reflecting the puffy clouds in the blue sky. Never again would he stroll hand in hand across this arch with Laikas. Kragan had reached into his chest and left behind a smoking hole.

Maybe a thirst for vengeance would soon fill that cavity, but for now, only a void remained.

31

As the last light of day gave way to a fiery sunset, Arn watched as the khan's son, Larok, and his horsemen departed for Val'Dep, taking with them Ty's body. It was wrapped in white linen and lay in a wagon pulled by a team of High Lord Rafel's finest oxen. Larok had given Ty's corpse the same level of respectful preparation as he had given to that of his own father, the khan.

Larok had insisted that Ty's body share the funeral of honor with his father, to be held outside of Val'Dep. Rafel had agreed. They had further agreed that High Lord Rafel and Earl Coldain would be present two days hence. The army of Tal would stand in honor of both Val'Dep's fallen khan and the man the horse warriors had named Dar Khan.

There was no doubt in Arn's mind that the riders of the khan who had seen Ty in battle believed that he was the Dread Lord, and Rafel would ensure that his people paid proper respect to that belief. Arn could never repay the debt he owed his Kanjari friend who had held the trail, trading his existence for Carol's. And in saving her life, Ty had saved all the people of Areana's Vale. Coldain had turned the tide of the battle, but his forces could not have fought their way into the vale in time to prevent the slaughter of all Rafel's people.

So, forty-eight hours later, on the wide parade ground of Val'Dep, Rafel and Coldain stood in front of a formation of twenty thousand soldiers of Tal, staring up at the pyramid dais of the khan as the sun sank over the western cliffs.

Atop the dais, the horsemen had removed the khan's throne and erected two wooden scaffoldings. One now bore the khan's body, and the other bore that of Ty. The people of Val'Dep spread out around the parade field that surrounded the dais.

On the outer wall of Val'Dep, where Alan had fought only days earlier, stood Arn, Carol, Alan, Kim, and John. As a thousand riders galloped from the city to slide to a halt in a great circle at the base of the dais, Kim's body shook with sobs, and tears ran freely down John's cheeks. Two riders jumped from their mounts with burning torches and raced up the steps to the top of the dais. Together they lit the wood piled at the base of the two funeral pyres.

A gust swept through the canyon, whipping taut the flags atop the city towers. The wind raced south, fanning the fire under the khan's scaffolding into a roaring blaze but snuffing out the fire beneath Ty's pyre.

The crowd stood in stunned silence as the fire consumed the khan's body in a glorious spectacle that lasted several minutes. But the swirling flames refused to spread to Ty's platform. As the khan's funeral pyre turned to ash, darkness descended. Storm clouds buoyed up across both rims of the canyon. Lightning crawled across the sky, a shifting, skittering web.

Suddenly three separate bolts arced downward, simultaneously blasting into the wood piled at the base of Ty's funeral pyre. The thunder that accompanied the strikes roared outward with a sound that shook the ground, a rumble enhanced by the monstrous blaze that shot up to consume the scaffolding on which Ty lay.

As the blaze grew in intensity, the clouds roiled overhead, wind rocketing around the fire so that it burned ever hotter, sending up a spiral of flame and ash.

The wind shrieked, forming a small funnel as the clouds themselves opened up, rain gushing forth that would have flooded the valley had the downpour not ended as abruptly as it began. The silence that cloaked the valley seemed louder than the turmoil of the storm. The top of the dais stood empty, swept clean by the fury of the winds.

In the distance, a lone stallion appeared atop the canyon, the palomino rearing high and pawing the air, sending forth a lonesome, piercing whinny.

As its echo died, another replaced it. *"Dar Khan!"*

The yell of a thousand horsemen was picked up by the women of Val'Dep and repeated so that the canyon walls and city battlements amplified the sound, making it louder than the preceding thunder.

Arn pulled his gaze from the dais and leaned over, his mouth close to Carol's ear. "I suppose you had nothing to do with that?"

Carol turned to him in wide-eyed wonderment. "I'm shocked that you could even suggest such a thing."

Strapped to Arn's side, Slaken grew hot. Arn grabbed for the burning knife, and as his hand closed on the haft, a pulsing heat spread through his blood until his temples throbbed, liquid fire coursing through his veins, knotting his muscles into cramps that brought him to his knees. A sudden vision filled his mind of himself and Ty in the caverns beneath Kragan's city, Lagoth, as they created a blood-bond with Slaken.

As Carol reached for Arn, concern etching her features, the torment passed.

Staggering back to his feet, he said, "It's okay. Just a moment of weakness."

Filling his lungs with a long drink of the cool evening air, Arn's eyes briefly met Alan's, seeing in those orbs the memory of holding Ty's body as he died. Then Arn gazed out over the scene below and swallowed hard. "Goodbye, my friend," he said, wiping away a tear. "Good journey."

Epilogue

Southwestern Endar
YOR 415, Late Spring

In his color-shifting uniform that blended with the hillside, Galad strode out of the kingdom of Endar alone, heading south through the Endless Valley, weaving time-mists around him. Queen Elan had tasked him with an urgent mission: to find High Lord Rafel and request his aid in the coming war with Kragan. Galad would also summon Kimber and Carol Rafel that they might fulfill their roles in Landrel's prophecy. It was a request that the high lord and his daughter would honor, just as his mother had answered such a request from Rafel decades before.

Now Galad just needed to find his half sister and her family. It was a search that would require weeks of travel. But ironically, the Endarians did not have the luxury of time. Kragan's army would reach Endar Pass in less than three weeks. It was the reason that Elan had sent Galad forth. He made the journey within a rychly mist while also creating a balancing pomaly fog trailing behind. Many weeks passed within the rychly zone, while in the normal world only a couple of days went by.

He could not constantly stay within the passage he had created since the normal world fogged over when he moved through the rychly mist. So Galad stepped through the fog to study the land ahead, then reentered the mist and covered the distance to the horizon. He repeatedly came out of the mist to reconnoiter the next stretch of terrain that lay before him. When he needed rest, he stayed within the rychly zone, sleeping as only minutes passed in the outside world.

Fortunately, his search was not a random one. Due to his blood connection to Kimber, he gained a general sense of her presence during his brief intervals outside the mists.

As the days became weeks, his sense of Kimber grew stronger, pulling him toward the Glacier Mountains in the southeast. And through constant use, Galad's mist-weaving skills improved. He no longer doubted that he would soon find his sister and High Lord Rafel. But one very big question remained.

Could Galad channel enough time-mists to bring Rafel's entire legion back to Endar with him?

—⁂—

The razor-sharp outline of the high mountains silhouetted against the moonlit sky to the west did little for Kragan's mood, serving only to whet his appetite. He moved silently across the hills outside the massive encampment where his forces gathered, fresh arrivals swelling their numbers with each passing day.

Beyond those mountains lay Endar Pass, the home of his soon-to-be-extinct enemies, the Endarians. His fury that several hundred of the time-mist warriors had managed to escape back to Endar Pass smoldered within his chest. He would soon quench that fire with Endarian blood as he purged their species from this world.

That day would truly be worthy of celebration, a day that Kragan's subjects would speak of in reverent whispers throughout all the ages to come. They would whisper his name instead of that of the prophecy's bitch.

Kaleal's voice echoed in his mind. *We should have taken care of Lorness Carol when she was weak from fighting. Such opportunities should not be missed.*

"No. I want her to come at me at full strength when we meet. I must have her in all her terrible sorcery and beauty. Only the clash of our powers can shatter the barrier the Endarians erected and open the whole world to me once more."

Kaleal's laugh boomed out over the war camp, causing men, vorgs, and other creatures to look about for the frightening sound's source. *Be careful what you wish for.*

—⟋⟍—

Far away in Areana's Vale, Arn lay naked, spooned up against Carol's back, his left arm encircling her. In the depths of her sleep, she tossed and turned, mumbling in her dreams, the last few words just loud enough for him to make out.

"Be careful what you wish for."

With gentle strength, Arn thought of what she had endured and hugged her close, whispering words of comfort in her ear. "Always, my love. Always."

ACKNOWLEDGMENTS

I want to express my deepest thanks to my lovely wife, Carol, without whose support and loving encouragement this project would never have happened.

I also want to thank Alan and John Ty Werner for the many long evenings spent in my company, brainstorming the history of this world, its many characters, and the story yet to be told.

Many thanks to my wonderful editor, Clarence Haynes, for once again helping me to refine my story.

ABOUT THE AUTHOR

 Richard Phillips was born in Roswell, New Mexico, in 1956. He graduated from the United States Military Academy at West Point in 1979 and qualified as an Army Ranger, going on to serve as an officer in the US Army. He earned a master's degree in physics from the Naval Postgraduate School in 1989, completing his thesis work at Los Alamos National Laboratory. After working as a research associate at Lawrence Livermore National Laboratory, he returned to the army to complete his tour of duty.

Today, he lives with his wife, Carol, in Phoenix, where he writes science-fiction thrillers and fantasy—including The Rho Agenda series (*The Second Ship*, *Immune*, and *Wormhole*), The Rho Agenda Inception series (*Once Dead*, *Dead Wrong*, and *Dead Shift*), and The Rho Agenda Assimilation series (*The Kasari Nexus*, *The Altreian Enigma*, and *The Meridian Ascent*). He is also the author of *Mark of Fire* and *Prophecy's Daughter*, the first two books in the epic Endarian Prophecy fantasy novels.